CW01662670

The In
Dame

Book Four: The Secret Diaries

Also in Sphere Books

THE INTIMATE MEMOIR OF DAME JENNY EVERLEIGH
BOOK ONE

THE INTIMATE MEMOIR OF DAME JENNY EVERLEIGH
BOOK TWO

THE INTIMATE MEMOIR OF DAME JENNY EVERLEIGH
BOOK THREE

The Intimate Memoir of Dame Jenny Everleigh

Book Four: The Secret Diaries

SPHERE BOOKS LIMITED

SPHERE BOOKS LTD

Published by the Penguin Group
27 Wrights Lane, London W8 5TZ, England
Viking Penguin Inc., 40 West 23rd Street, New York, New York 10010, USA
Penguin Books Australia Ltd, Ringwood, Victoria, Australia
Penguin Books Canada Ltd, 2801 John Street, Markham, Ontario, Canada L3R 1B4
Penguin Books (NZ) Ltd, 182–190 Wairau Road, Auckland 10, New Zealand

Penguin Books Ltd, Registered Offices: Harmondsworth, Middlesex, England

This novel is a work of fiction. Names, characters, places and incidents are either the product of the author's imagination or are used fictitiously.

Any resemblance to actual events or locales or persons, living or dead, is entirely coincidental.

First published by Sphere Books Ltd 1988

Copyright © Potiphar Productions 1988
All rights reserved

Printed and bound in Great Britain by
Richard Clay Ltd, Bungay, Suffolk
Set in Monophoto Sabon

Except in the United States of America,
this book is sold subject to the condition
that it shall not, by way of trade or otherwise,
be lent, re-sold, hired out, or otherwise circulated
without the publisher's prior consent in any form of
binding or cover other than that in which it is
published and without a similar condition
including this condition being imposed
on the subsequent purchaser

Plaisir d'amour ne dure qu'un moment,
Chagrin d'amour dure toute la vie.

Introduction

This often salacious yet always entertaining chronicle, first published some one hundred and twenty years ago, may well shock today's reader by its graphic, undraped descriptions of a variety of sexual encounters.

This book certainly shows us a completely different side to the traditional portrait of the social life and times of Victorian Britain. That the age was stuffy to a point almost beyond belief is not challenged by modern historians. Rightly, we still associate the period with a smug, often aggressive puritanism which valued perhaps even to the point of fetish the concept of 'female purity'. To spare the ladies' blushes, piano legs were discreetly covered and simple, everyday articles of clothing like 'trousers' were bowdlerised into 'unmentionables'!

A gospel was preached of sexual abstinence and of celibacy as a desired state and even within marriage only the minimum bedroom activity was allowed and that was for the sole purpose of procreation and in no way simply for pleasure!

An obvious corollary from this unnatural suppression of the prime biological drive was of course no small measure of sexual deviancy and dysfunction especially amongst the burgeoning numbers of the bourgoisie who thought that these 'genteel' attitudes were those of the aristocratic classes whose way of life the nouveau riche were attempting to ape. It is no mere coincidence that during the nineteenth century flagellation (a deviancy often arising from arrested sexual growth) became known rather contemptuously as *le vice anglais* on the more enlightened European Continent. Most modern therapists would agree that the giving and receipt of pain to stimulate sexual desires often comes from repression of juvenile sexuality such as the perfectly normal adolescent discovery of masturbation or even the simple 'wet dream' which naturally occurs among (and often worries) young teenage boys.

Interestingly enough, women were believed to possess no sexual passions (and if they felt twinges it was their duty to suppress them!) but Dame Jenny's diaries are proof of the rebellion against that notion which appears so ludicrous a century or so after its propagation. Now we all smile at the classic anecdote of the Victorian mother giving advice to her daughter the night before her wedding – 'lie back and think of England' – but to many Victorian girls, without knowledge and kept ignorant as far as possible about their own bodies let alone of any male appendages, this was all they could expect of the marriage bed. It was their lot to put up stoically with men during their 'baser moments' but for an unmarried girl, one act of sexual intercourse led to her 'ruin' for she was no longer in that so highly prized precious state of virginity.

These were unyielding axioms and caused much distress to both men and women alike and as such were ridiculed in much of the material that made up the popular underground magazines and booklets of the 1870s and 1880s. Here, in a sometimes rough and uncompromising fashion, the joys of sexuality were asserted, and perhaps those publications owed their undoubted popularity to their unashamed efforts to create an acceptable place for sexual behaviour in the lives of their readers and to assure them that sex offered the greatest joys to be found.

Although we know that a female had penned Dame Jenny's diaries, regretfully we will never know the true identity of the writer. For 'Dame Jenny' quite reasonably hid her identity under the cover of a pseudonym. The first and less explicit volumes may have been written by Mrs Belinda Heather (1848–1931), one of the first of the new breed of scribblers who scratched a living from the growing number of mass market publications which began to appear around 1880.

We have no clues as to the identity of the girl who wrote this and the following books except that she was known to Sir Lionel Trapes (1826–1908) who mentions Mrs L. 'alias Dame Jenny' in his own journal, noting how much amusement they afforded his 'friends of both sexes'. Trapes, whose own secret biography cries out to be written, was himself a leading light in the 'fast' yet ultra fashionable South Hampstead set led by Doctor Jonathan Arkley who along with Trapes was a good friend of H. Spencer Ashbee, the doyen of Victorian collectors of gallant literature.

The booklets in which the diaries first appeared were at first thought to have been published by the mysterious D. Cameron who was responsible for the spectacularly rude underground magazine *The Pearl* in 1879. But Professor Timothy Shackleton, a modern authority on nineteenth century erotica, is of the opinion that they were probably published by Philip Yale, a wealthy South London printer of 'French postcards' who specialised in photographs of *poses plastiques*, the Victorian equivalent of today's page three pinups.

'Dame Jenny' eschews the grosser perversions of her age – child sex, incest and sado-masochism – though a liberal tolerance pervades her diaries. She would doubtless have agreed with Mrs Patrick Campbell who just a decade later was to comment on the hounding of Oscar Wilde that consenting adults should have the right to do whatever they wanted in bed 'so long as they didn't do it in the street and frighten the horses'.

Her robust vitality comes across the years through her lusty narrative, especially in this selection which contains some of the frankest yet evocations and descriptions of a variety of sexual acts. Sir Lionel Trapes, whilst noting that 'Doctor Jonathan (Arkley) attended Mrs L. – the celebrated Pepys of *l'arte de faire l'amour* – and we are all delighted at her excellent recovery from influenza', also wrote of his concern that she cavorted too enthusiastically as syphillis was running rife at that time and was as incurable then as

AIDS is today. Even or perhaps especially for someone like 'Dame Jenny', the concept of safe sex was as valid then as it is in our own liberated age.

Godfrey Elton-Stanton
Cockfosters
May 1988

Why should I not publish my diary? Many famous people are named in its pages and if I revealed the nomenclature of just a few of those (of both sexes) who have enjoyed intimate relationships with me, London Society would be horrified and the cross-Channel ships would be quite crowded the very next day with the cream of Kensington ladies and gentlemen who had suddenly decided to take the Grand Tour or even spend the next few years in France!

I have not hesitated to name those who I know will not flinch from what some may feel to be astonishing or even scandalous exposure. But my dear, dear friends of the calibre of sweet Lady Charlotte C**** or the staunch Captain Peter M*** need spend no sleepless nights racked with uncertainty as to whether I shall unlock the secrets that could cause this memoir to be perused with anguished care amongst the very highest in the land.

So I shall remain, with your pardon, gentle reader, cloaked in a somewhat transparent veil of semi-anonymity though I shall not even attempt to hide the pleasures of delicious voluptuousness that I have enjoyed ever since I discovered the joys of *l'arte de faire l'amour*. False modesty is as foolish and vulgar as overweaning pride and I will admit at once, as I turn back the pages of memory to my eighteenth birthday on August 3rd, 1871, how fortunate I have been to be blessed with a body that has always enjoyed sexual excitement and has also possessed the ability to arouse similar sensations of the flesh in those who have wished to join me in the delights of licking and lapping, sucking and fucking.

Are my words too direct for you? I warn you now that I make no apology for whilst I have little time for mere crudery, there have been many occasions in my life when, for the sake of simple accuracy if nothing more, only such rough language could convey my true, unembellished thoughts at the time the events described took place.

So let us begin our journey with the frank recollections of what happened on a very special railway journey. A final note of introduction: as with all following entries in my secret diary, these words were written almost without exception within forty-eight hours of the happenings they describe.

August 3rd, 1871

I have always enjoyed travelling on the railways. Even when I was a child of tender years I never drew back from the edge of the platform when the engine came huffing and puffing into our little station of Etherbridge that was just one and a half miles from Grandpapa's country estate in Dorset.

Yes, dear diary, I just KNEW that today, my birthday, would provide me with some interesting material to insert in my diary although little did I dream what else might be inserted – and where!

I am composing this essay in bed at Aunt Portia's house in Sloane Crescent at the end of a day which has transformed me from a shy virgin into a woman of the world. So without brooking any delay, let us start, dear diary, at the beginning of the fun when Grandpapa helped me into the first class compartment of the London train which was already occupied by two pretty, if demure looking girls of my own age.

I waved my farewell as we chugged out of the station and began to climb the steep incline towards Postle Junction. It was not without pride that I noticed one of my travelling companions eying me. This caused me no concern as frankly I enjoy being looked at and I smiled as I fumbled in my bag for the book I planned to read on the three and a half hour journey.

What is sauce for the goose is sauce for the gander, I thought to myself as I snuggled down in the comfortable seat. So I glanced to my left where the two girls were sitting next to each other. Though I have often been complimented upon my full figure, unblemished skin and pretty ringlets of fine golden hair that come tumbling down when I let my hair free from pins and brooches, I had to admit that in beauty, the girl in the emerald green dress (none of us wore our coats, which had been given to the care of our respective servants travelling in the third class carriages at the rear of the train) was indeed my equal. She was of dark complexion, rather slender of figure but with well proportioned breasts and languid hazel eyes. Her lips were a succulent shade of red and when she laughed at an amusing remark from her friend she showed pearl white teeth that sparkled in the sunlight that poured through the windows of the compartment.

Her companion too was attractive to view – she was perhaps a trifle older, nineteen or even twenty perhaps. She was a lovely rosy-cheeked girl with a merry twinkle in her blue eyes which were of the same brightness as my own although my hair is certainly a shade or two lighter in colour. She wore a fashionable royal blue dress, nipped in at the waist which accentuated her large breasts which were obviously encased only by an exquisite white silk blouse which I was later to learn had been bought in Paris by an admirer.

The dark haired girl noticed that I was looking at her and she smiled sweetly across the carriage.

'Hello,' she said with a friendly grin, 'is it not a delightful day we have chosen to travel to London? I take it that you will be accompanying us to Paddington?'

'Yes, indeed I am going all the way,' I replied, 'and I am quite excited as I have never been to London by myself before.'

'May I ask what takes you there?' said the other girl.

'I am going to be introduced into Society,' I said, 'as my

own dear parents are even now undertaking a far longer journey than we three to the United States of America to see my sister who married an American gentleman two years ago and is now expecting a new arrival in the family.'

'Wait a moment!' said my first new found travelling companion. 'Is your name Jenny? I am sure we were introduced at General Petty's Spring Ball just last April. I remember listening as you told Johnny Oaklands about how your parents would have to visit New York this summer.'

'Why, of course!' I cried. 'But you must forgive me as your names escape my memory.'

'No need for forgiveness, Jenny,' chimed in the elder girl.' My name is Yvonne Mainwearing and this is my best friend Lizzie Wright. We are also going to London for the Season but our parents are already in their town houses. For the first week we shall be staying with Madame Kooshay who runs the Female Equestrian Society For Ladies of Quality.'

'Of course we can both ride jolly well,' laughed Lizzie, 'but we asked for lessons at Madame Kooshay's establishment as one can meet some lovely young men there! Don't tell out though, Jenny, or we'll all be in trouble.'

'Heavens, I won't say a word to anyone,' I declared and we began chatting away as we girls are wont to do. Lizzie had a picnic basket and we shared some cucumber sandwiches and drank, I am ashamed to say, two bottles of claret.

We were now all sitting together with me in the middle. Of course, we were now all very relaxed and I felt just a wee bit tired and I rested my head against Lizzie's full bosom as the train pulled sharply around a curve. I pulled my head away but Lizzie said: 'No, no, Jenny, do leave your head on my breast. It is most comfortable for us both.'

Nothing loath, I let my head rest and I must have drowsed there in that position for some ten minutes. I recall the train stopping and then pulling out of a station and hearing

Yvonne whisper: 'Let's do it now, the train won't stop until we reach Swindon and that won't be for almost an hour.'

I then felt myself being gently lowered and my feet being brought up from the floor so I was lying on my back with my head still cushioned by Lizzie's soft body though now I was using her tummy as my pillow.

'Isn't it too hot for comfort?' said Yvonne and I nodded sleepily in agreement. And then to my astonishment I felt my dress being unfastened and before I could summon up any serious resistance, my dress was off and I was covered only by a bodice and petticoats. I was now wide awake and as Lizzie stroked my face, I could see Yvonne hastily divesting herself of her clothes until in a trice she was naked and I could admire her slender, lithe body with its pert white round globes with dark brown nipples that looked almost impudently large as she stroked them up herself until they stood out like hard little corks. Beneath them at the base of her flat belly between her legs lay a mass of glossy black curling hair, extending all over her mount and even hanging down a little between her thighs.

Yvonne smiled at me and gently climbed up on the seat to kneel, quite nude, between my legs which she parted to make room for herself.

'I am sure that you have a gorgeous cunt, Jenny,' she said softly, 'you don't mind if I see if my fancy is based upon fact, do you?' And before I had a chance to say whether or not I did object, the saucy young minx quickly raised up my petticoats exposing my belly and thighs to her lascivious gaze. Then as Lizzie continued to stroke my face, Yvonne placed her hand upon the fine covering of blonde hair that covered my own delicate notch. She then began to massage my thighs. The experience was not exactly unknown to me as we had played with each other in the dormitory at St Hilda's School, but Yvonne's busy fingers made my heart quicken and my whole body quiver with desire.

I felt totally uninhibited as she played with my little pussey, pulling open the love-lips and rubbing her knuckles back and forth across the entrance to my already moistening crack. Then as she eased a finger into my cunt, I began to sigh and raised up my bottom, gasping and trembling all over at the exquisite sensations as now one finger was joined by another and then a third as Yvonne began to finger fuck me at an ever increasing pace.

Yvonne now moved up over me, still keeping her fingers working inside my oozing pussey, and she kissed me passionately on the lips. A velvet tongue slithered between my lips to make contact with my own as my arms wrapped themselves round the sweet girl. At the same time Lizzie had quickly divested herself of her garments and padding round us, jumped behind Yvonne, whose firm, splendid bum was sticking out as she leaned over me, frigging my cunney with her left hand and running her right hand over my breasts, bringing my nipples up to a fine state of erection. I opened my eyes to see Lizzie part Yvonne's legs and then, twisting herself round so that like me she was lying on her back between my legs, Lizzie placed her mouth at the entrance of Yvonne's glossy haired mons Veneris and began to lick and lap round Yvonne's cunt to send the girl into paroxyms of delight.

My buttocks tensed again as Yvonne's fingers plunged in and out of my warm, juicy cunney. They poked around and around inside and every now and then she toyed with my erect, pulsating clitoris. Oh, it was such blissful agony! I seemed always to be on the verge of coming but she would stop just in time and hold back the waves of orgasm that threatened to swamp over me. But I could hold out for only a little longer and indeed I welcomed the release as I groaned and twirled around as my spend came gushing down over Yvonne's clever fingers and my saturated clitty sent shudders of pleasure all over my body as I climaxed quite beautifully, reaching the highest pinnacle of pleasure.

I lay back exhausted as Lizzie and Yvonne, still quite nude, scrambled to their feet and stood embracing in the passage between the seats (whose arm rests had been thoughtfully put up by Lizzie, as I should perhaps have mentioned earlier). Their lips were glued together as they rolled towards the seats opposite and lay down with Lizzie on top.

Yvonne lay flat on her back but Lizzie cupped the wriggling cheeks of the lovely girl's bum, bending forward to suck greedily on her engorged, stiff little nips, leaving them though to be tweaked and caressed by Yvonne's own hands as Lizzie slowly kissed her way down Yvonne's marble white belly to the black cushion of glossy black hair that guarded the entrance to the haven of her pussey. Lizzie licked her lips in anticipation and her pink tongue extended itself, moving slowly abut the puffy cunt lips causing Yvonne to sigh and gasp with unashamed delight. Slow and subtle in her ministrations, Lizzie parted the lovelips with the very tip of her wicked little tongue. The joyful, fluttering tongue now sought the moist cleft where already (though I could not see it) Lizzie's clitty was already swelling.

'Oooh! Oooh!' cried Yvonne, cradling Lizzie's golden locks in her hands. 'Suck harder, darling, suck harder and make me come!'

Lizzie responded at once, clutching those magnificently firm bum cheeks as she thrust her face deeper between Yvonne's legs, sucking and slurping with great ardour, rolling her tongue round and round, lapping up the sweet love juices which were now freely flowing from Yvonne's juicy cunt.

'Aaaah! Lizzie, darling! Oooh, your tongue is like a little cock fucking my pussey!' cried the exquisitely pretty girl.

My blood was up and my fingers strayed down towards my own slit, burying themselves as far as they would go as I began to frig myself whilst watching the two tribades continue their love-making to the final thundering climax.

'What a gorgeous cunney you have, my dear, dear Yvonne! Oooh, such a glorious pussey and how cleverly it sucks in and presses my tongue. If only I had a cock I would like to fuck you myself!' said Lizzie, bending over again to recommence her tonguing of Yvonne's hot, wet cunt. She continued to pass her tongue lasciviously around the most sensitive parts and as I moved closer to watch, the serrated vermilion cunney lips slightly parted and between them I could see her stiff fleshy clitty that projected quite two inches and which was as big if not bigger than my thumb . . . Lizzie took that glorious clitty in her mouth, rolling her tongue around it and playfully biting with her teeth. Then, receiving one last sweeping of Lizzie's clever little tongue, Yvonne began to spend. Her hips bucked violently, her back rippling, and then from her longing pussey spurted a fine, creamy emission that flooded Lizzie's mouth with its milky essence.

'Ooooh!' Yvonne screamed in ecstacy, grinding her crack passionately to Lizzie's open mouth whilst yet again and again the bliss repeated itself until she found herself swooning away until finally shuddering into limpness, heaving and panting with exhaustion as the delicious crisis ebbed slowly away.

My fingers were still busy frigging my own sopping cunt which was spending and throbbing under the titillation but then the train whistle sounded and I withdrew my hand from my pussey in panic. Goodness gracious, whatever could we say if the train were to make an unscheduled stop and someone was to open the carriage door! My heart began to thump, my head was swimming wildly and for a moment I thought that I should faint clean away! I would never even see London now but would find myself, horror of horrors, as a prisoner at the police court!

Fortunately, my dear friends quickly had a solution to hand which was not surprising of course as they had surely fucked together several times in railway carriages and they must have been accustomed to unwanted interruptions.

'Pull down the blinds, Jenny,' ordered Lizzie. 'Yvonne, you look after the other side so we shall be safe from prying eyes from across the tracks. Be swift!'

We did as she commanded, and Lizzie grabbed hold of

the door knob to prevent anyone else entering the compartment. Fortunately for the three girls, corridors that enabled passengers to move from compartment to compartment had not yet been introduced although their arrival was imminent. Railway employees could move along the train by using a narrow exterior catwalk that ran alongside the coaches, but passengers who wished to change compartments could only do so via the station platforms.

'I cannot understand why we should be slowing down,' muttered Yvonne. 'We are not scheduled to stop for something like twenty-five minutes. I trust that we shall not be delayed.'

Lizzie's eyes lit up as she cried: "Oh, heavens, I know what is happening. Jenny, this is all because of young Johnny Oaklands who we saw at the ball where we were introduced. How could I have forgotten that he wrote to me last week to say that he was coming to London for the Season and would try to arrange his trip so that we could meet on the train. His uncle by marriage is the Belgian railway magnate Monsieur Harold le Meshigunah and the British railways would do anything to make Monsieur le Meshigunah invest in their companies so Johnny can just join the train where he likes, as long as he gives sufficient notice. Why, I doubt if he even has to pay a fare!'

'I didn't know the Oaklands were in trade,' said Yvonne a mite disparagingly.

'I don't think that matters a jot,' said Lizzie warmly, 'but as it so happens the Oaklands are of course a country family of the highest rank, being closely connected through Johnny's grandfather to the Shropshire Kirkin-Naylands and through the maternal line to the Duke of Dorset, who is of course connected to my own family through Uncle Teddy.

'However, Johnny's mother's youngest sister, Fanny, married this queer foreigner – and I understand that he really is a rum cove, being of Turkish extraction which accounts for his somewhat strange name. He is frightfully well-off, though, and I know that Johnny wants to meet him in town to see if the beggar will help to meet some of Johnny's expenses. His father keeps Johnny on a tight rein as he says that his son spends too much money on wine and women, which of course he does!'

We laughed merrily at her words as the train slowed to a halt. We heard a man's tread coming closer towards our carriage. The footsteps stopped and the man outside knocked twice on the window which I had covered with the blinds on Lizzie's instruction.

An aristocratic young voice shouted: 'This is Friern Mount Station, Miss Lizzie Carstairs, and this is Johnny Oaklands here. I know it is you in there, Lizzie, so open the door and let me in.'

'Very well, Johnny,' replied Lizzie, 'but come in quickly.' She opened the door just wide enough to let Johnny in and swiftly closed the door behind him. He was carrying a small case as no doubt his servant was struggling with the heavy luggage further down the train. 'What the deuce!' he said. 'Lizzie, why on earth have you drawn down the blinds on such a beautiful summer day?'

He was about to say more when simultaneously the train lurched forward to recommence our journey and Johnny gasped with astonishment as his eyes, now accustomed to the darkness after the bright sunlight outside, took in the fact that standing giggling before him were three lovely girls all without a stitch of clothing to their name! I modestly covered my hairy mount with one hand and laid the other across my breasts. Yvonne impudently placed her hand over Lizzie's sleek blonde bush whilst her friend returned the favour. No wonder, the handsome young man could hardly believe the evidence afforded by his own eyes!

He stumbled down onto the seat as the train gathered speed but it was several seconds before he regained any substantial amount of composure – and who could blame the lucky young devil who had had no prior knowledge whatsoever of just how eventful this railway trip to London was going to be.

'I don't believe my eyes!' he gasped. 'I must be hallucinating. It's this damned hay fever. Nothing excites my hay fever so much as the dust of a stagecoach. Yet though my eyes were streaming with tears before, they are clear now. No, no, I am imagining this!'

'Are you imagining this as well?' said Lizzie, an impudent hussey of the first order, as she leaned forward, stroking her large breasts lasciviously just inches away from the handsome boy's face.

'And are you imagining this, too?' laughed Yvonne, settling down on her back on the seat in front of him, opening her legs and taking my own unresisting hand to place over her moist mons Veneris.

Johnny laughed as the train driver blew his whistle as we chugged merrily at full speed.

'No, I don't think I am imagining anything at all. It appears to me that I am going to enjoy a superb if unexpected birthday present, especially as we shall not be stopping till Reading.'

'Is it your birthday, Johnny?' I asked.

'Yes, Jenny, today I am nineteen years old.'

'Then you deserve something very special,' I said, and taking my hand from Yvonne's wet crack, I rubbed my hand against the bulge already forming between Johnny's legs.

Well, as you can imagine, the young spark needed little more encouragement than that and he undressed as quickly as he could with some help from the three of us.

Oh, but what a handsome young man was Johnny! His finely chiselled features, his twinkly hazel eyes, his little moustache setting off a strong manly countenance! And his beautiful body, such a beautiful body! I needed to possess that virile frame, his broad hairless chest, his slim flanks and shapely legs and that monster purple headed prick that rose so majestically from between his legs up to his belly-button, leaving exposed those soft, hairy balls that I took gently into my hand when, as if in a dream, I kissed that red-topped truncheon and Johnny caressed my head in his hands as I fondled his darling cock, positioning the head so that I could envelop it in my mouth.

This was not the first time I had sucked off a naked cock but fear of pregnancy had led me to keep my cunney only for my own or (since the start of this journey) for feminine fingers.

But my blood was up and as I sucked lustily on Johnny's cock I decided that I must find out for myself the joys of fucking.

My period had only just finished and though I know how foolish it is to fuck unprotected, I knew that I just had to have that gorgeous prick inside my pussey.

Lizzie must have been reading my mind for she said very tenderly: 'Jenny, dearest, I can see that you want Johnny to fuck you. Don't suck his prick any more or he will not be able to stop himself spending.'

'Lie down upon the seat and I will place his fat cock in your cunt to your mutal satisfaction,' she added sweetly.

I did as I was told and by the sparkle in his eyes I could see how well Johnny took to this suggestion though he said nothing except to moan gently as I gave his prick one final lick and kiss.

I laid down on my back and noticed that Yvonne was gently frigging herself and I could hear the squishy sound as her fingers slurped in and out of her cunney.

Lizzie took Johnny's throbbing cock in her hand as she then bent over me putting her blonde tresses between my legs as she began to lick my pussey. I felt her lips parting the lips of my cunt and I was in raptures as immediately she found my excitable clitty which sent me twitching with desire. My cunt was now spending under the voluptuous titillations of her velvety tongue. Aaah, the memories of the moment!

But there was better to come as she lifted her head and

motioned Johnny to lie on top of me. She made him put his hands besides my burning face and to lean forwards on his forearms so that most of his weight would not be upon me. And as his body sank slowly down, she took hold of that grand, dazzling cock and gave it a final rub to bring it to its maximum length and breadth. Now I felt the hot head of his cock placed to the mark. The ruby head was lodged in the entrance but so huge was the erection that even with all the stretching my cunney had recently received, it would not enter despite the ample flowing of my love juices,

Johnny drew himself back to wet the knob as darling Lizzie gently opened my cunney lips with one hand and with the other guided the glistening knob till it was fairly lodged just within the portals of that tight yet luscious mouth. Slowly and gradually he pushed his way in. It did not really hurt me though I could not say that the experience was hugely pleasurable until, in my excitement and desire to be a woman, my bottom pushed out to meet his thrust and – such joy – without much pain, my hymen was torn and as Johnny guided his lips to mine, sucking in my tongue in the most ardent possible manner, we commenced a most marvellous act of intercourse.

At first he moved slowly until my sated pussey, awash now with mingled juices and blood, held Johnny fast, spurring him on to a faster pumping as I held his cock tightly, feeling his foreskin drawn backwards and forwards at every shove.

How I enjoyed my first fuck! The knowledge that I had finally crossed the Rubicon added a piquancy to the enjoyment, I am sure, and as I screamed from excess of emotion as I spent, I felt his copious emission of creamy spunk gush into my womb. What a sublime moment! I seemed transported to another me, I was indeed in Paradise, swimming in a sea of pleasure, in a perfect agony of bliss.

Johnny lay still upon me, exhausted for the moment by the profuseness of his tremendous gushing spend.

Naturally, the sight of our lovemaking was most

stimulating for Yvonne and Lizzie who were by now entwined on the long seat opposite, laid at full length but in reverse position so that each other's head was between the other girl's legs!

Yvonne's dark mane covered Lizzie's silky blonde mount but Johnny reached out to move Yvonne's hair to one side as she raised her head slightly and we could see her pink tongue lapping at Lizzie's stiff little clitoris which projected quite two inches out of her vagina. Yvonne sucked it with relish, playfully biting the excited clitty as Lizzie wriggled and rolled in absolute delight as she herself inserted her own tongue into Yvonne's sopping pussey, licking and lapping her in a superb double gamahuche. Their well-rounded bottoms bounced and twisted until Yvonne lay on her back sucking upwards into Lizzie's dripping slit whilst the pretty blonde pushed forward to nuzzle Yvonne's cunney, giving Johnny and I a magnificent view of her perfectly formed, enticing bum cheeks.

Johnny's thick cock had begun to rise and I decided that I must repay my debt to Lizzie. He must have known what was in my mind in much the same way as Lizzie had herself earlier correctly ascertained that I desired Johnny to fuck my virgin pussey.

With one bound he leaped up behind Lizzie, and in a trice his arms were about her, tweaking her hard little nippies that stood out so delightfully against the creamy whiteness of her snowy white breasts. His cock was now rock hard and I affectionately stroked the foreskin up and down the throbbing shaft that bucked against my palm as I circled the base of the awesome tool. And almost simultaneously, as if knowing what was planned, Lizzie lifted up her glorious young bottom slightly parting her legs to allow a better view of the beautifully wrinkled tight little brown bumhole as Yvonne continued to gamahuche Lizzie's cunt with her wickedly busy little tongue. I now wet the top of Johnny's cock with my tongue and slipped the knob into my mouth. I opened my jaws as wide as possible to suck in as much of that great prick as possible until it almost touched the back of my throat.

I now withdrew and carefully, with my hands, directed Johnny's rearing cock to her bottom crack. I stroked Lizzie's flushed cheeks as she continued to suck Yvonne's sopping cunney whilst her hips jerked at the first nosing of Johnny's cock into her arsehole. A startled cry and a febrile twitching of her juicy bum cheeks as his cock made its first acquaintance with the sphincter muscle, forcing its way in between those glorious buttocks, meant that the proceedings had now begun in earnest.

'Aaaah, aaaah!' cried Lizzie. 'Ooooh! Oooh! Your cock is too big. Oh! Oh! Oh!' But he was now in, and resting just for a few seconds, began his fucking motions. I could tell from the excited wrigglings of her bottom that Lizzie actually did enjoy being cornholed. His hands were busy squeezing those succulent nipples whilst Yvonne never left ministering to Lizzie's cunt. This was another fervent engagement; the two girls gamahuched each other with the most erotic ardour whilst Johnny's excited cock revelled in the tight-fitting fundament of the exquisite Lizzie who wriggled and plunged about so excitedly that I worried about the three of them falling off the seat and onto the floor especially as the carriage was rocking slightly as we rattled along the line.

How excited they got, until each seeming to spend at the same moment, they screamed almost in unison in the frenzy of emission. The combination of emotions from both her cunney and bumhole quite carried Lizzie away in a divine rapture, melting away into a sea of lubricity.

After Johnny had withdrawn his now dangling semi-limp cock, Lizzie jumped up leaving Yvonne lying panting on the seat. 'I still have to spend,' she wailed. 'It would be most unfair to leave me so.'

Johnny and Lizzie stood aside to let me take their place on top of the ravishing girl who lay nude on the seat. How the sight of her swelling breasts heaving up and down with passion made my senses quicken and excite. I lay down, pressing my warm body against Yvonne's. Our tongues met and our hands passed beneath each other's soaking pusseys. I kissed the mounds of her firm breasts that jiggled under my lips and drank in the beauty of the springy black curls of her mount that showed up against the pure sheen of her belly where her thighs dipped in so enticingly.

'Is it not so nice to kiss and be a little naughty?' murmured Yvonne. I nodded my assent as I passed up one hand to her right breast and fondled the swelling titty. Peaking ardently to my touch, the nipple quivered erect as she sighed as I continued with my other hand to frig her dripping cunney, letting two, then three, then four fingers slide in and out causing her to gasp with desire.

She moved her hands up my sides and we embraced, breasts pressed against breasts, belly against belly. I recommenced to frig her soaking cunt, slowly but deliberately opening the velvet folds then rubbing the moist lips as she shuddered with pleasure. I felt her hard little clitoris and feeling it quiver against my touch, swept my head down to lick and suck her juices as she moved her torso upwards so that she could cup my breasts in her hands, flicking my nipples into hardness. Spreading her cunny lips with my tongue I readjusted my head for comfort and relaxed into flowing movements with my tongue nudging her clitty, pushing against the hood. Yvonne's legs clasped my head as she thrashed wildly from side to side, squeezing and pinching my breasts sending ripples of delight speeding down to my own cunt and to our great joy we soon brought ourselves to that delicious state of annihilation which causes the soul to dissolve itself in an ocean of bliss.

We had only a short time to rest from our labours before it was time to put our clothes back on. However, we three girls decided that we had to give Johnny a final birthday gift so we took turns to suck his cock. I was fortunate enough to be sucking his thick prick when he began to spend. A veritable flood of spunk jetted between my eager lips. I swallowed the salty white cream that flooded from his wonderful tool, greedily extracting the last drops as the feel and taste sent spirals of pleasure spinning through my body.

So I am now a woman and I have no regrets about the way I have lost my virginity which was becoming a burdensome state. I am glad to have lost my hymen. Perhaps I should be ashamed to confess this but here lies the advantage of writing a diary. I may confess anything I like and nobody can think any the worse of me. My conscience may be eased quite comfortably and my failings, such as they are, may be examined as severely as desired. Yet I still possess the luxury of not being found out. So I have all the advantages of a conviction without the nuisance of a penalty. Decidedly, this writing is a great easement of the mind.

We were not disturbed by any other passengers until we reached Paddington. We spent the time in idle talk though I was quite impressed when Johnny told me of his interest in chess. I knew he was a dashing young sportsman but I associated his recreation with more active country pursuits such as hunting, shooting and fishing.

'Yes, Jenny,' said Johnny, 'I am particularly keen on chess, which I find most stimulating as an indoor pursuit.'

'Oh, surely not so stimulating as fucking!' interrupted Yvonne, at which we all burst out laughing.

'Well, fucking is far more stimulating to my cock than chess but my brain does crave for other perhaps more cerebral activities. I am hoping for a game or two against Professor Nathan Wabolowski, the great Russian master.'

'Is he a good player?' I inquired.

'Most certainly one of the best in the world. I shall be privileged to play with him for he will easily beat me. But I shall learn from the experience and it will be a match that I shall remember all my life.'

'Didn't I read somewhere that a great American chess expert has just died?' said Lizzie.

'Yes,' said Johnny. 'You are referring to the tragic death of Mr Paul Morphy. The Obituary notice in *The Times* last Thursday must have caught your attention. He was only forty-seven years old and when he was just twenty-one he came to Europe and beat practically every European expert. I think he even took a game from Nathan Wabolowski.'

'Oh, you are familiar with Professor Wabolowski?'

'Actually he is more friendly with my father,' admitted Johnny. 'But it would be most helpful to my plans if I could effect an introduction to the Professor for Monsieur le Meshuginah, my dear old uncle. I know he would be very pleased and show his appreciation with some much needed cash! The problem is that the Professor is somewhat of a recluse for he is terribly busy writing his autobiography.

'Indeed, he is only seeing me this evening as my father wrote to him to say that I was coming up to London and that today is my birthday. As it is, he has promised me only an hour of his time between five and six o'clock,' added Johnny.

My goodness, it is almost half past three in the morning! I will be so tired when Aunt Portia comes to wake me up. Never mind, I don't think she has much planned for the day. I will plead a headache and stay in my room till luncheon. Johnny has invited me to partake of afternoon tea with himself and Professor Wabolowski.

It seems the Professor enjoys the company of young girls – which is just as well as I cannot play chess! Perhaps I can arrange for Hudson, our butler, to send out for a book on the game. After all, I should not wish to be thought of as a complete *ignoramus*. Well, I am so sleepy that I must say good night, dear diary, or rather I should say good morning!

August 5th, 1871

Dear diary, you must excuse the lapse of an entry for yesterday but I was quite too exhausted partially because of all the entries of another and, it must be admitted, a far more exciting kind with which I was involved. Let me take up the story from yesterday afternoon when Aunt Portia's coachman, Graeme, took me in her carriage to Albion Square, Bloomsbury, where the Oaklands family rented a house for the London Season.

I dismissed Graeme and told him that Mr Oaklands would be escorting me home later that evening and to remind my aunt that I would not be dining at home tonight.

Albion Square was not, perhaps, in the fashionable part of the West End of London. But the houses were of excellent design as was evident in the delicate tracery of fanlights over the doors and the wrought-iron balconies that broke the plain fronts. Johnny told me later that it was the balconies and the small but pleasant back gardens which had induced his father to rent a house here.

And although the gardens may have been too small for serious entertaining, in compensation, the inhabitants of Albion Square were free to use a railed oval of grass fringed with evergreens. It made a lovely patch of summer greenness and, as the gates were locked and other householders (many of whom were elderly people) were apt to mislay the keys, and the spiked railings were high enough to thwart stray urchins, there was seldom anyone inside this enclose and there was little traffic to disturb the peace.

Johnny opened the door himself and to my surprise, seemed to be dressed solely in a white bathrobe. How fortunate that one of Aunt Portia's eccentricities was to allow me out without a chaperone!

'Heavens! I know the weather had been exceedingly warm this afternoon but surely we cannot take tea with Professor Wabolowski dressed or rather undressed like that!' I said, as Johnny ushered me into the front room.

'We are not going out,' he laughed, 'and the good Professor is coming over here so there is no need for formality.'

'But what about the servants?'

'My maid, Janette, has left everything prepared and I have given her the rest of the afternoon off to say farewell to her gentleman friend.'

'That is very kind of you.'

'Well, she is a very conscientious girl, trustworthy, discreet and absolutely honest. A real treasure, in fact, and anyhow I think the chap she has been seeing is a bit of a cad. He promised her an engagement ring but I have a suspicion he is already married. I have only seen him once but he looked like a bounder to me.

'Anyhow, a matter of more importance is that we are alone,' he added, 'which is why I am greeting you in this state. I have just taken a most refreshing cool bath and allowed myself a splash of cologne which I find most invigorating.'

I should have guessed from that moment, if not before, should I not, dear diary, what that robust young fellow had in mind!!!

If truth be told, as indeed it must in these pages, I was not exactly unprepared in either mind or body for concupiscence despite the rather uncomfortable heat.

Without further ado, I lifted up my pretty face to be kissed and as we embraced I could feel his sturdy tool rising against my belly. I kicked off my shoes and helped Johnny to take off the rest of my clothes until I was clad only in my Italian linen shift.

I slid my hand across his chest as he shrugged off his robe and pressed his body even closer to me. I took hold of his bare cock and as soon as my hand was around it the shaft began to throb and jerk.

I was already very wet and when I pulled his prick between my legs, I held him in position so that my cunney lips just touched his knob and I rubbed his knob along and on to my clitty. The effect was shattering and I wanted his cock inside me immediately. Fortunately, we were practically the same height, which makes it easier to fuck while still standing up. Even so, the feel of his darling cock pushing into my cunt almost buckled my legs. Waves of pleasure swept through me so that I had to put my arms around Johnny's neck to balance myself, pressing myself as close as possible, my inflamed naked breasts welcoming the cool of his manly chest.

To steady me Johnny put his hands round my bottom so that he could ensure his prick was in me to the very fullest extent. The superb sensation of its vibrating length allowed me to enjoy a shuddering spend even before he began to actually fuck me.

I was inexperienced, perhaps, but my body knew that we were doing all the right things with our hands. He squashed my supple bum cheeks whilst with one hand I caressed his neck and with the other, his perfectly shaped balls. It has been said by many (including Lady Belinda F******* who should know better than any woman in London) that older men are better at fucking but Johnny was a gentle and skilful lover and whimpered with pleasure as his cock kissed my juicy pussey and the shaft of his divine prick rubbed so teasingly against my trembling clitoris.

We moved in a drunken fashion towards the couch and I pushed Johnny down so I could place myself on top of him. For an aching moment, his cock left my cunt but quickly I was positioned kneeling naked in front of his bright eyes. He massaged my firm young breasts as I slowly lowered myself onto his rampant cock. I took Johnny's balls in my hand as I moved myself up and down on his rock-hard tool. But to my astonishment he moved my hips upward and took out his glistening wet prick – but only to slide me further up his slim torso so that he could rub his mouth against my cunney lips.

He pushed his tongue right through the lips which made something explode inside me. I moaned with delight as his tongue moved in quick circles over my clitty.

'Aaaah! Oooooh!' I thrashed around on the couch as one demented. 'Oh, Johnny dearest, please fuck me. Put your sweet cock in my cunt, there's a dear.'

Ever the gentleman, he obliged me and changing positions, I laid on my back to receive his shaft that slid wetly between my legs between the portals of paradise to rest momentarily in its favourite home. Johnny now began to fuck me with long, slow strokes, gradually increasing the tempo until he rightly judged that we both desired to spend and began to pump faster and faster as we approached the point of no return.

Suddenly his body stiffened and I could feel his climax approaching with mine. He exploded into me in a rush of liquid fire. With every throb of that big cock, more spunk shot into me, mingling with my own love juices till I thought it would never stop. My own orgasm came instantly as my saturated clitty sent ripples of bliss throughout my body.

But this delightful boy had not finished! His cock remained stiff inside my cunt, indeed if anything even harder than when we began! I gently eased him out and he replaced his prick with his tongue flicking in and out of my honeypot causing even more spurts of juice cascading out of me as he greedily slurped my spendings into his mouth.

I manoeuvred myself round so that his stiff cock bobbed enticingly in front of my face. I placed my hands around the base of the shaft and took the pulsating purple knob into my mouth. It was not too easy and I had to stretch my jaw to get it in and to quiver as I sucked lustily on my lollipop but I did not wish to draw him immediately into another exhausting spend.

So I pulled his prick out of mouth, holding it level with my lips, gripping firmly to prevent it springing upright. The juices were oozing out of the tip to be instantly lapped up by my darting little tongue. I then pulled my head away but it was too late. I now know that sucking the shaft and flicking the knob of a prick make a man spurt very quickly.

Johnny continued to kiss and suck my cunney as his

creamy jet of spunk came hurtling out of his prick. The first jet hit me on the cheek. My head went back to enable me to gobble furiously on this jerking cock and his spurting knob rested on my tongue, held there by my right hand. I had to swallow quickly to keep pace with him. Then, as his spend passed its peak, I took his whole cock back into my mouth and sucked for all I was worth to extract the very last drops of spunk from his pumping prick.

We lay silent for a spell, exhausted by our frenetic passions. I declare that Johnny would have been happy to stay in my arms for the rest of the day (and I would have been equally as happy for him to do so) but I reminded myself with a start that we had a distinguished guest arriving soon to partake of afternoon tea!

'Come now, my dearest,' I said with some determination, 'we must be in the right frame of mind to receive our distinguished guest.'

'I think nothing would please the good Professor more than if we received him *au naturel*,' demurred my handsome young boy, 'as I do understand that after chess, Monsieur Wabolowski's great passion is fucking.'

'Johnny! How could you say such a thing,' I exclaimed. 'I would have thought the Professor would be far above such business!'

'Oh, my dear sweet girl, how naive you are! Fucking is the most important business in the world for any man. All that differs between members of the male sex is the fierceness of their drive and their choice of fuckee. Some prefer plump girls, some slender, some young and some mature. And of course there are some who prefer to fuck each other although I feel sorry for the sodomites as they are missing out an awful lot of pleasure for an activity I would imagine to be damned painful!'

'And where does Professor Wabolowski fit into your pattern?' I asked.

'Oh, Nathan has a strong sex drive. And he is very, very fond of sweet young girls of eighteen who fuck with passion!'

'Is he now! I suppose you would like me to fuck the Professor so that he will entertain your rotten relation, Harold Le Meshigunah? After all, that would be a certain way to ensure that you keep your annual compliment from Harold.'

'Gosh,' said Johnny excitedly, 'I hadn't thought of that. Oh, no, my darling Jenny, I couldn't ask you to take on the thickest prick in London just to keep me in the style to which I have grown accustomed.'

'The thought never entered your head?'

'With my hand on my heart, I can say it never crossed my mind,' said Johnny, 'although I suppose you might enjoy the experience.'

'And how would you feel?' I enquired, for by now I knew that I was blessed with a higher sexual appetite than most and could easily be persuaded to offer sport with the Professor if what Johnny had said about the chess master's prick were true.

'I must be candid with you,' said my bright young spark, 'for it has for some time been my delight to fantasise about a troilistic engagement.'

I wondered if he had been telling me the full truth beforehand, but I decided to give him the benefit of the doubt and without further ado, I suggested that we entertained the Professor in the bedroom.

Just then, there were two knocks on our front door. But it was not our honoured guest but Janette, Johnny's maid, returned from saying goodbye to her gentleman friend.

Gathering up my clothes, I retired to Johnny's bedroom and lay down on his most impressive four poster, idly wondering how many girls had been fucked there when to my surprise, Johnny walked in with Janette just behind him.

'Janette has given me this note from Professor Wabolowski. He will be about half an hour late but looks forward to his visit,' said Johnny, apparently unconcerned that I was lying down on his bed quite naked.

I looked up modestly only to be surprised again. For there was Johnny, passionately kissing his maid, who was obviously relishing the experience.

Janette was a pretty young thing, perhaps eighteen like me or perhaps a year my junior. She was somewhat sallow of complexion with dark brown hair over a rather low forehead but with a most pleasing expression of face. Her large sparkling eyes promised sultry pleasures and I confess that a thrill ran through me as Johnny unlaced her corsets, fully exposing a beautiful bosom, ornamented with a pair of lovely rounded globes, with dark nipples, and her skin, although so white, contrasted well with our fairer complexions.

She was soon denuded of every piece of clothing and Johnny playfully pushed her onto the bed next to me. What a beautiful girl she was with nicely proportioned limbs but such a glorious profusion of hair, that from her head, now let loose, hung down her back in a dense mass and quite covered the plump bum cheeks. Idly, I caressed her thighs and let my hand stray between her legs into the mass of bushy brown hair that covered her warm, moist slit.

This dalliance continued as her hand now wandered to my titties which she expertly flicked into a hardness with the palm of her hand. I was now becoming excited myself and I felt the juices trickling out of my pussey. Without a word, Janette rose up, knelt in front of me and then in a flash her head was down, nuzzling between my thighs. I expected it and lay perfectly still, enjoying the sensation as her busy little tongue twirled around inside me. Second by second I could feel my cunney moistening the more, delighting in the ripples of pleasure as she plunged her tongue in and out of my now dripping slit, teasing the labia that sat exposed, ready through the net of fine fair hair, flicking past it, gently licking and sucking until I was in a frenzy of lust.

'Ooooo, oooooh, that's beautiful,' I cried, 'now please, pull my clitty and make me spend!' The dear girl wrenched her mouth from my sopping muff and replaced it with her long, taping fingers. Immediately, she found my swollen clitty and tugged it vigorously and before long my body began thrashing wildly about in a frenzied ecstacy as she slid a finger into my bottom-hole. I felt like exploding as my back arched upwards as spasms of excitement ran throughout my body exploding into a gigantic peak of orgasmic lust.

I hauled the delicious girl up into my arms and crushed

her plump, soft breasts hard against mine, our tawney titties rubbing against each other as we kissed deeply and feverishly until a second eruption made me arch back again crying our in joy as the raging storm of my spend coursed through me.

Janette lay back, no doubt expecting me to perform a similar service for her and I would willingly have done so but the little scene I have described had so excited Johnny that he could not forbear to wait a moment longer, and shucking off his robe plunged his naked frame between us. He gathered me in his strong arms and I reached down for his bursting, stiff cock as our mouths met and our tongues waggled against each other as we kissed with the utmost passion. I rubbed his shaft up to its peak, gently pulling his shaft up and down and marvelling at the size of this huge, naked cock. I pulled my mouth away and kissed his chest and moving quickly downwards with a series of butterfly kisses, soon found his throbbing prick. I opened my mouth wide, wetting my lips to take in the red, bulbous head as Johnny groaned with delight.

I pushed downwards until his massive cock was at the back of my mouth and I sucked and slurped on this lovely lollipop of a cock. I jammed my mouth over the mushroom dome and sucked happily away until his prick began twitching uncontrollably and I felt the creamy white spunk would soon be rushing up the shaft and yes, yes, yes, my mouth was filled with gorgeous gushing foam as his cock bucked wildly as I lightly held it between my teeth. I gulped down all the liquor from Johnny's magnificent cock, sucking up every last milky drop of cum.

What with our previous escapades only a short time before downstairs, this was too much for my young feller-me-lad and he almost swooned back onto the bed, his great velvety prick now shrunken into submission though I correctly guessed that this was but a temporary state of affairs.

It was my turn now to have my way with lovely Janette. I rolled over on top of her and we kissed hungrily. Her mouth was moist and hungry. I licked her nipples up to a fine state of hardness and let my eyes feast upon her hairy cunt. The dark brown hairs were crisp and well fluffed-up and the lips looked oily with the excited thoughts she had apparently sustained whilst I was sucking off Johnny. I went over her entire body with my mouth and tongue as she sighed and let her arms pull me closer towards her.

She was a most shapely creature and as she murmured her pleasure as I worked my tongue into the whorl of her navel, she reminded me of a sleek, pampered cat as she stretched out her legs and languidly arched her back, silently imploring me to explore between her thighs. I rubbed the flat of her belly and let my fingers linger in the crisp hair of her mound. The skin of her pussey was marvellously soft and damp and I was amazed at how easily my forefinger slid into her cunt and how smoothly it could work in and out.

Still frigging slowly into her cunney, I kissed her belly and worked downwards to her hairy mound. My lips slithered downwards until they were directly over her quim and I could taste the warm, rich cunney juices which were flowing freely from her. I parted her legs to ease my head down into a comfortable position and plunged my pointed tongue back and forth in her pussey. Janette squirmed and moaned, pressing up into me, almost threatening to suffocate me with her hairy muff.

'Lick me, lick me, don't stop now,' she gasped as for an instant I paused in my ministrations.

She need not have been concerned as I had no intention of ceasing to suck that delicious cunt. My tongue slid through her smooth passageway and outlined the mound of her clitty, rising up to greet me. I lapped all around it, this coming as an inspiration and proving most effective as she began to stir, her legs waving this way and that as my tongue continued to slurp until I took that pulsating clitty in my mouth, rolling my tongue around it and nipping it gently with my teeth. Now she squealed with delight as I worked my tongue until my jaw ached but soon the lovely girl heaved violently, her back arched and she came in a fierce spurting as my hand slipped under her comely bum and I worked my forefinger in and out of her arse in a most exciting way. I sucked her cunt until her orgasm faded away and then we lay entwined in each other, releasing the last drainings of juices which mingled in an oiling of our thighs.

Our reverie was interrupted by a thunderous knocking on our front door.

'Help! It must be Professor Wabolowski,' I cried.

'Don't worry, ladies,' advised Johnny, slipping into his robe and a pair of slippers. 'I'll warn the Professor what to expect and I'm sure that he will join in the fun.'

'Who is this man?' asked Janette nervously.

I explained the situation to the trembling girl who brightened visibly when I told her that the good Professor was reputed to possess one of the biggest cocks in Old London Town. And Janette, being a loyal servant, was quite happy to be fucked by Professor Wabolowski should the need arise, for she was very fond of Johnny and in any case she received liberal wages which Johnny could only continue to pay if Harold Le Meshigunah continued to fork out the necessary cash.

We heard the murmur of voices and then Johnny threw open the door and the nude charms of two pretty girls were fully exposed to the gleaming eyes of Professor Wabolowski.

He was a large man of about forty years of age, and must have been at least six feet three inches in height with luxuriant red hair and a trim yet full beard setting off a pair of twinkling grey eyes and a somewhat prominent curved nose.

'The blonde lady is Jenny Everleigh and the dark haired girl is Janette, my faithful maid,' said Johnny, undoing the belt of his robe and climbing naked onto the bed.

I was startled at my own presumption as I added: 'Won't

you join us, Professor? You look quite hot and bothered standing there. Take off your clothes and we shall cool you down.'

'Later, that is,' added Johnny with a merry laugh.

'My, my,' said the Professor in a charming Continental accent, 'I had come here under the impression that we were going to play a game of chess but perhaps there is another game to be played, no?'

'Another game to be played, yes!' I cried, quite reckless now with abandon. 'Come on, Professor, throw off your clothes. I want to see the biggest prick in London.'

'For that you must view Jumbo the elephant in the Zoological Society gardens in Regent's Park,' beamed Professor Wabolowski, 'but you are welcome to trifle with my own instrument of pleasure.'

In a trice he was as naked as us. His chest was covered with the red hair of his beard and his corpulent belly sagged a trifle without the power of his clothes to pull him into shape but his cock – merciful heavens, what a massive truncheon stood out from the morass of red hair that covered his pubic area! His cock was truly enormous, at least three inches longer than Johnny's and certainly thicker. Jenny and I gazed in awe at this fearsome weapon whilst Johnny looked on with no doubt mixed emotions of jealousy and admiration. I put out my hand to stroke this huge cock as the good Professor clambered up onto the bed and I suddenly realised that there was something strange about this monster tool. As I pulled my hand up and down the ivory shaft, I realized that the twitching purple dome was totally uncovered and that there was no foreskin to pull back.

'Is there something wrong, Jenny?' said Johnny, noticing a slight furrowing of my brow.

'Not really,' I said, 'but I hope you will not take offence, Professor Wabolowski –'

'Call me Nathan, my dear Jenny,' interrupted the Professor.

'Very well, Nathan, I hope you will not mind but may I ask if you have suffered an accident with your cock?'

'An accident?' said Janette, bending over to plant a wet kiss on the mushroomed bulb. 'Why, what's wrong with this fine prick?'

'Well don't you notice, Janette? The Professor, I mean Nathan, doesn't seem to possess a foreskin,' I said with a note of surprise in my voice.

At this both Johnny and Nathan burst out laughing.

'What is so amusing?' said Janette crossly. 'Jenny is quite correct, I can see for myself that this cock is different to any other I've seen and I have seen quite a number if only to toss them off for I am very selective about the boys I let fuck me. I hope the lack of a foreskin does not mean you have been diseased, sir?'

'No, no, no,' spluttered Johnny. 'You may rest easy on that score. Have neither of you seen a circumcised cock before? You both surprise me as there are quite a few around fashionable Society.'

'I have never seen such a cock as this, though it is not displeasing to the eye,' said Janette. 'I suppose it must be nice fucking and being sucked or tossed off without a foreskin to get in the way. But it must have been a most agonising operation to undergo. Was it worth such pain as the experience must have been quite shocking.'

'No doubt it was, my dear,' said Nathan with a chuckle, 'but as I was only eight days old when the cut was made, I remember absolutely nothing of it.'

'Nathan is Jewish,' explained Johnny, 'and all Jewish boys are circumcised by religious officials known as *mohels*.'

'What a job to do with such responsibility,' said Janette idly, licking her lips before jamming her mouth over the purple knob and sucking up Nathan to a fine cockstand.

'It doesn't pay too much,' said Nathan, gasping with emotion as Janette's hand cupped his huge, hairy balls as she continued to suck lustily on this giant penis which rose majestically up from between Nathan's legs.

'No, the wages aren't good but the tips are great!' chortled Johnny, whose own prick was now waving frantically skywards and demanding a share of attention. I smiled my appreciation at his witticism and grasped Johnny's cock which though not the size of Nathan's was of goodly proportion. I leaned over and took the purple bulb into my mouth, sucking and nibbling my lover into a ramrod straight erection.

Then I leaned back, glancing at Janette who was still slurping noisily on her giant tool, and pulled apart the lips from my juicy cunt which glistened with anticipatory lust. Johnny moved quickly, sliding himself on top of me and we kissed passionately, moving our thighs together until our pubic muffs rubbed roughly against each other. I grasped his cock and ran the head up and down over my slit and he only had to push gently and he was inside me, stretching the walls of my love sheath.

'Fuck me, Johnny,' I whispered. 'Fuck me nice and hard like only you know how to, you randy boy.'

I arched my back up to him, begging his thick prick to enter my welcoming depths. He pushed in as far as he could making me yelp with pleasure. Then he started to push in and out and I felt the muscles of my cunt tighten and I grasped his buttocks to me and I felt his breath on my shoulder as he thrust that lovely cock in and out of my juicy cunney. Now my hands roved across his broad back and I dug my nails into it as his large balls banged against my bumhole. We fucked beautifully in a glorious rhythm of long slow movements in perfect unison. As my own body felt the sexual tide begin to build he increased the speed of his thrusts.

Now I was about to explode and I burst into a torrent of fiery sensation as his cock throbbed violently inside my sopping cunney and then, oh! the ecstacy as he shot his seed inside my womb as we erupted in a quivering mutual climax. Our joy was matched just inches away where Janette had just begun to suck the flowing spunk that was pumping out of Nathan's stiff, jerking prick. She lapped delightedly at the white froth that came bubbling out of the tiny 'eye' of that massive knob. She smacked her lips as his libation finally ended and said: 'I do love the taste of spunk. I am sure it is as good for my health as the most invigorating of tonics. And of course, I can never get my belly swollen up this way!'

The arms of Morpheus await me – it is long past midnight and I am too tired to write fully of the later excitements of that marvellous day – so I shall lay down my pen, dear diary, and continue this epistle immediately after I wake up. I do hope Aunt Portia will remind the servants to work quietly and let me sleep until late morning.

August 6th, 1871

I did not wake up until eleven o'clock this morning much to the concern of Aunt Portia who warned me not to overtax my strength as the Season was upon us and I would find that perhaps all too soon, life would be all balls.

With difficulty, and in deference to my dear aunt's spinsterish state, I resisted the strong temptation to reply that this was indeed already the case as far as I was concerned!

Mind you, dearest diary, I must confess to have often wondered whether my amiable aunt has ever enjoyed the pleasure of taking a prick between her legs. She is unmarried, true, yet being my mama's youngest sister, she is only thirty-eight years old and is generally reckoned by the family to be a most attractive woman. And this reminds me, diary, that I must find time today to compose a letter to my parents who are visiting my two brothers Nicholas and Austin in the New World. Both the boys are taking long vacations from their labours (such as they are) and I am sure they are having a fine old time in New York City.

But I digress and must return to Johnny Oaklands' elegant apartment in Albion Square.

After we had recovered from this enjoyable sexual encounter, it obviously occurred to Nathan that whilst it was most enjoyable to have one's cock sucked, there was still a greater pleasure to be enjoyed, namely in actually have a fuck.

Despite his foreign background, Nathan's manners were impeccable. He tapped my shoulder gently and asked me if he could have the honour of inserting his cock inside my cunt. Johnny looked on a little anxiously as I dare say thoughts of what might happen with regard to Monsieur Le Meshigunah if I declined crossed his mind. However, he need not have worried as I had no objection whatsoever to being fucked by Nathan and his giant circumcised cock.

I smiled my consent and I lay back to enjoy the exquisite feeling of Nathan's cool hands stroking my breasts, then he bent his head and a sublime feeling flowed around my excited nipples as he worked his tongue over them, raising them up to hard little bullets, moving expertly as if he had always known my body.

Now aroused, I worked my fingers down his hairy chest, stroking a trail across his tummy down his glistening cock and I saw the glistening dome rising urgently as I grasped the stiffening shaft. He buried his face in my breasts and at the same time his hand drove down between my legs and his thumb and forefinger opened my already wet cunney lips. He scrambled up into a kneeling position and I was forced to let go that gorgeous tool which was as hard yet smooth as ivory. But I was compensated as I clutched at his head, now snugly encased by my thighs, and I moaned my approval as he pressed his lips down upon my wet pussey.

Mouth to cunt, he sucked every fold, slipping his clever tongue through the pink lips and my cunt was now gushing love-juice. Each time he tongued me my clitty stiffened, even more eager, wanting more and more as his mouth responded to my jerking passions, engulfing me completely. Now I needed Nathan inside me and I pulled his head away from the honeypot. He raised himself up and gently lowered his frame upon mine, one hand holding his luscious cock which he carefully laid across my burning slit.

'I need you inside me, Nathan, fuck me with your big cock and make me spend!' I cried out.

Nathan made a deliciously slow and sensual entry as I raised my legs high to wrap them round his torso. His succulent rod buried its throbbing length full within my cunney and his heavy balls couched themselves beneath my bottom. My cunt was delighting in this thrusting prick that slid so effortlessly in and out in such a sensual way. His pumping quickened as my bottom arched up to receive him and he clasped my white bottom cheeks as we fucked and fucked like a couple possessed, his long, thick prick working backwards and forwards in my sopping pussey. I tightened the lips as best I could and squeezed the muscles, all the better to feel the ridging of his knob.

My cunt was now on fire as a raging orgasm shuddered through me and I knew that Nathan's moment of truth was near. I felt his body go rigid and I felt a copious wad of sperm come flooding into me. He shot once, twice, thrice and his spunk spurted out with such intensity that I could imagine it splashing off the rear wall of my cunt. Indeed, so abundant was his jetting that my bush and thighs were lathered until, still tingling sweetly within me, his fervent cock at long last withdrew and rubbed itself amorously in a last salute against my sticky cunney lips.

Watching our sport had sent the blood coursing through Johnny's veins and he was now sitting up alert with Janette kissing and sucking his erect shaft. She must have begun this action whilst we were still fucking, as Johnny groaned with delight as the pretty girl rubbed his shaft with a quick motion and his creamy white froth spilled out from the top of his sturdy stem to be lapped up in style by Janette who sucked up every last drop of spunk until his cock began to droop downwards.

'Are you busy this evening, Nathan?' said Johnny. 'It occurs to me that we could dine early and it would be my pleasure to take you and the two girls of course to the Adelphi. Jenny, it is some time since you have visited the theatre, is it not, whilst Janette here has probably never seen a real play as she has only been taken to the music halls.'

'I have made no arrangements and it would give me great pleasure to accompany you,' said Nathan.

Jenny and I were most excited and we kissed Johnny most affectionately. Janette and I later luxuriated in the pleasures of a warm bath though the men preferred to take cold showers. Johnny had secretly planned the evening's excursion and had hired Monsieur Le Meshigunah's coach for the evening, slipping Connor the coachman a sovereign for his attendance. Monsieur Le Meshigunah himself would probably have made no fuss as he was in Manchester concluding some important business and was not expected back for at least another day.

We ate a light supper at a very smart new restaurant, Le Monaco, and swept into Johnny's box (well, actually it was booked under the name of Monsieur Le Meshigunah!) just before curtain up.

I thoroughly enjoyed the play, 'The Silver Falls', which was a strong, healthy melodrama with vice and crime rampant in the first two acts but brought to their knees in the last. It was a stirring story with a fierce, Borgia-like adventuress, a confederate scoundrel, a deserted lover and a weak fool of a husband.

The deluded husband had been trapped into matrimony by a seductive field and he allows himself to be pillaged by the rogue simply because they were schoolfellows. But when his wife's villainy is unmasked he repairs to Mexico, goes through a lot of adventures in that cut-throat country, is a sort of king amongst the miners and of course meets the virtuous heroine with whom he straightaway falls in love and everything eventually happens that should happen. But the cruel wife has followed him to Central America and claims him as her husband on the eve of his betrothal. In the end, though, all comes right as the dagger of an old lover frees our hero and almost at the same moment a letter announces the death of an uncle and his accession to the title and lands of Lord Avondale. Really and truly a very good play with plenty of excitement, very pretty scenery and good acting, especially by Mr Charles Cartright as the scoundrel friend of the wicked wife. I mentioned this to Johnny as we snuggled up together in the carriage that would make its first stop at Sloane Crescent where old

Newman, Aunt Portia's faithful old retainer, was no doubt waiting for me to return so that he could lock up the house for the night.

'You like the look of Charles Cartright?' said Johnny.

'Well, you must admit that he is a most handsome man,' I replied.

'It so happens that I have played cricket with him. If you like I will invite him round to tea.'

'You have played cricket with an actor?' I said. 'I am not a snob but I would not have thought that Mister Cartright would be found in your social circle.'

'Actually, Cartright comes from a very decent family. He is regarded as the black sheep, as you would imagine, by his folks for taking up a career on the stage, but in fact we were at Eton together.'

'You were at Eton?' said Janette, who was snuggled up against Nathan, one hand lazily rubbing his monster cock which she had taken out of his trousers. 'My sister, Florrie, worked there for a term.'

'Of course she did, we've all heard of Floreat Eton!' laughed Johnny although naturally Janette did not understand Johnny's clever word-play.

I was now quite tired and Johnny alighted with me as we came to a stop outside Aunt Portia's house. I wished Nathan and Janette good night and Johnny escorted me to the front door where old Newman was already standing. I gravely shook hands with Johnny and he told me that he would call round at noon to take me to luncheon if I had no other arrangements made by my aunt. I told him that to the best of my knowledge the day was free and I felt really sleepy and indeed my eyes closed the moment my head touched the pillow.

August 8th, 1871

I have been so busy by both day and night that I do not believe that I need excuse myself for not composing any entries for the last two days. It is, of course, the other entries of a most intimate nature that have kept me away from your pages, diary, but I shall keep nothing back as I confess to enjoying so much transcribing the pleasures of the flesh down in your secret pages. So only a cursory note of apology for this hiatus of two days and let me now straightaway record what transpired the day after I went to the theatre with Johnny, Janette and Nathan.

My beau called for me exactly on time – I was later to learn of his pleasing propensity for punctuality – at noon. Aunt Portia had not objected to my going out for the day as she herself was busy attending a meeting for the Committee for Universal Suffrage at Lady Ossulton's fine Mayfair home in Park Street. More of my aunt's radical political philosophy will no doubt be espoused during my stay.

Anyhow, to return to my narrative, Johnny had again borrowed the Le Meshigunah carriage though he warned me that the owner was expecting to dine with him tonight and perhaps I would come with him to lend moral support.

'Will Nathan meet Harold Le Meshigunah and consent to play chess with him?' I asked anxiously.

'Heavens, yes. That is all sorted out and I must thank you and Janette for providing such a feast of erotic entertainment for our good Professor. Nathan enjoyed himself so much that I knew he would not withhold his consent when I put the matter to him. I am taking Harold over to Nathan's Gray's Inn Road apartment tomorrow morning and hopefully Harold will feel himself in my debt.

'I must see if I can persuade Father to augment my allowance,' added Johnny, 'I don't enjoy having to skip round Harold to pick up the crumbs from his table.'

'How much does your Papa allow you, dearest?'

'Oh, a thousand a year and the Albion Square rent is paid for by my Uncle Edwin. I know the amount is generous but you would be surprised, Jenny, how quickly money flows through one's fingers.'

'You must count your blessings, Johnny,' I said firmly, 'as I think your family is quite indulgent. You are to study at Cambridge University from September, are you not? Your allowance will keep you there in the very lap of luxury,' I said warmly.

'I must admit that is so,' grinned Johnny with a roguish grin. 'It is the temptations of our Metropolis that cause me to overspend my income. But enough of this, Jenny, let me tell you where we are going. We are off to Hampstead Heath, well just a mile or so north of that fine expanse to Lord Holne's magnificent mansion. He has fifteen acres round his home and has laid out a superb private cricket pitch.'

I was not to be disappointed especially as the weather remained so fine. Connor covered the ten miles or so in good time and we enjoyed a fine alfresco luncheon with a small gathering of people all from the very top drawer of Society. The two teams that were in opposition were Lord Holne's XI against The Penguins, a scratch side to be sure but which contained one or two very well-known players such as Mr Cuthbert Smith of Sussex, Mr A. P. Lucas of Essex and two or three other gentlemen who have donned white flannels for their native counties. Lord Holne's team, on the other hand, was made up mostly of colts, one or two still sixth form schoolboys and others studying at Oxford or Cambridge Universities.

'Charles Cartwright is playing for Lord Holne's team,' said Johnny, passing me a glass of champagne, 'and as I recall they were at Eton together. I won't forget to introduce you during an interval. The players will be out very shortly and I understand that The Penguins won the toss and will bat first so we shall have the opportunity of seeing Charles in the field.'

We ate a delicious meal of mayonnaise of salmon, moist lobster and baked chicken all washed down with ice-cold champagne. Johnny and I sat together on a hammock sofa and settled down to enjoy the game. It was an elegant sight and I caught sight of Lady Elspeth Howcott, Mr Yerborough, Lord Lawrence and Major Norris amongst the distinguished guests who languidly clapped Lord Holne's team as they strolled out to take the field. 'Charles,' called out Johnny, 'we are over here, old man.' The tall, gracefully slim young man acknowledged Johnny's greeting and sauntered over to greet us.

'May I present Miss Jenny Everleigh, about whom I wrote in my note delivered to you early this morning,' said Johnny.

'I am delighted to make your acquaintance,' said Charles Cartright in that attractively strong, melodious voice that I had heard to such good effect the night before at the Adelphi.

Somewhat shyly, I smiled a return greeting, looking at his handsome face with its clear blue eyes and wide, generous mouth which he opened to reveal pearly white teeth that sparkled in the bright sunlight. I gazed down his body and took in his slender yet masculine frame and to my amazement noticed a swelling between his legs. But I said nothing as Johnny wished him good luck in the game and promised that we would meet him after the game.

I decided to broach Johnny about the bulge between Charles' legs. Surely he could not be having a cockstand just being introduced to a strange girl and anyway his mind was doubtless busy with the game that was about to commence.

Johnny choked back a laugh as he sipped appreciatively at his glass of champagne. 'Jenny, my sweet, you certainly notice matters of importance. But you are quite right, it is not a stiff prick that is causing the protuberance between Charles' legs but his cricket "box" which all players wear to protect themselves against a hard ball hitting their bollocks! These protective boxes are most necessary especially when facing the bowling of someone like Algy Barley over there who skittled out six players when he played last week for the Gentlemen of England against Middlesex at Lord's. Most players only wear boxes when they are batting but as Charles fields quite close to the bat at short leg, I don't blame him for not taking any chances.'

The Penguins' opening batsmen were George Gunn and Paul Attewell. Both had played for Oxford University and set about the bowling with a flourish. Poor Charles and the other fielders were sent scurrying all over the field although their running, throwing and catching were of a high order. This was cricket of a standard far above the level I had been used to back home. Those were real old-fashioned matches between neighbouring parishes where each attacks the other for honour and a supper, where laughing and shouting permeates the air. Here, it was very different, as boundary strokes were applauded only by a mere languid handclap. Anyhow, the score had reached sixty-nine (always a propitious number) when Attewell swung mightily at a loose ball which shot off his bat straight at Charles' belly. He bravely attempted to take a catch but the force of the powerful shot sent the ball clean through his hands right into his lower tummy.

We heard Charles cry out in agony and as he lay doubled up on the ground clutching himself between his legs, I agreed that it was indeed fortunate that he had decided to take the field wearing his protective box. The rest of the team clustered round Charles who appeared to be in dreadful pain. Johnny told me to wait a moment and he ran onto the field to confer with our host. A minute or two later, Johnny and Lord Holne helped Charles off the ground to the accompaniment of a sympathetic round of applause.

'Jenny,' shouted Johnny as they came near to me, 'I've been asked to field as a substitute. We'll take Charles into the house and I'll change into his togs.'

'Let me assist you, my lord,' I cried, rising up out of my seat, 'I will take your place at Mr Cartright's side to enable you to continue the game.'

'That is dashedly civil of you, Miss Everleigh,' drawled Lord Holne. 'Are you sure you will be able to manage? Here, Charles, put your weight upon Johnny Oaklands, yes, that's right. Now Miss Everleigh, let Charles put his arm round your shoulders and there you are – not too heavy is he?'

'Oh, no my lord,' I said truthfully, 'I can manage quite well.' And even if I had been in trouble, I would not have admitted it as I did enjoy having Charles' arm draped around me.

'You are too kind,' murmured Charles, as we staggered into the house and through into a large study. I demurely retreated and waited outside the door for the boys to change clothes. I did not have to wait long for Johnny soon appeared togged up in Charles' cricketing shirt and trousers. 'Perhaps you would like to go inside and comfort Charles,' suggested Johnny as he strode out to take his place on the field.

I had every intention of so doing, whatever Johnny might have said! I closed the door softly and saw the handsome boy, lying bare-chested on a big Chesterfield sofa. He grinned a welcome at me and for the second time that day, I noticed a swelling bulge between his legs. And this time, Charles saw the direction of my gaze.

'Why Charles,' I exclaimed, 'you silly boy, you have forgotten to take off your protective box!'

'No, I did not forget to take it off,' he said in that marvellous sultry tone, which caused me to feel a sensuous thrill tremble throughout my body. 'Would you care to see what lies behind the bulge?'

And before I could utter a word of reply, this forward

young man took hold of my soft hand and placed it firmly on top of his straining staff. I opened the buttons of his trousers and out sprang his swollen cock, sturdily rising upwards, slightly curved but as smooth as satin to my touch as I slipped his foreskin down to uncover fully the ruby coloured dome. I rubbed the shaft up and down, making the red head swell and bound in my hand. The sight of this succulent prick, which was longer than Johnny's but not so thick, set my cunt on fire and I resolved to get possession of it there and then. I helped Charles undo the buttons at the back of my dress and in a trice I stood naked in front of him, kneeling to keep frigging his satiny smooth cock and I saw myself handling his affair in a large full-length mirror that had conveniently been placed there (by Johnny and Charles when they changed clothes, of course).

I was indeed a pretty girl – well, false modesty is as foolish and stupid as overweaning pride – and my blonde hair, now undone into long tresses, veiled yet highlighted my full, firm breasts. My bare bosom was rising and the swell of those young bubbies acted as magnets to Charles' hands as he squeezed the globes and rubbed the tawney, taut nipples up against his palms until they were as firm as tiny bullets.

It was most stimulating to see each other quite nude in the dress mirror. There was I, first kneeling on the floor, then rising up to sit on Charles' lap, now kissing him violently on the lips whilst my hand stole up and down his long shaft whilst his hands roamed all over my curvaceous body. Then, shaking clear a fringe of blonde hair from my face, I bent downwards to take his rock-hard cock in my mouth. I sucked slowly, tickling and working round the little 'eye' on top of the bulbous dome whilst Charles parted my unresisting thighs and inserted two fingers into my moist, longing cunney.

Charles could see that my blood was up and lost no time in placing me on my hands and knees on the Chesterfield sofa, and wetting my bum-hole with ointment from a box on a side-table, made me push my bottom well out behind. I did as asked and turned my head to see Charles anointing his prick with the same pomade.

'Oh, Charles,' I faltered, 'I have never had a cock up my bum before. I hope you will not hurt me.'

'Fear not, Jenny, you will discover the most delightful channel of bliss and open up your senses to a ravishment of which you have hither had no conception.'

He angled my legs further apart to afford a better view of my wrinkled little nether-hole, but despite his promise, it did hurt somewhat when the head of his pick, which was fortunately not so thick as others I had entertained, entered the tightened orifice. I gasped with pain at his advance. 'Oh, oh, no, no more I cannot bear it,' I exclaimed. But the sphincter muscle gradually relaxed and I could soon enjoy the delicious frigging of my titties as he drew his arms round me, pushing firmly yet gently with his cock so that the initial pain gave way, as Charles had forecast, to a most extraordinary and delightful sensation as his movements stirred me up to the very highest pitch of excitement. His cock rose in and out of the tight sheath of my bum-hole, plunging in and out of the now widened rim, pumping and sucking like the thrust of an engine. I reached back and spread my cheeks even further and my bum jerked to and fro in time with Charles' rhythm until he shot jets of spunk deep inside me as we spent together in perfect accord.

Charles withdrew his still stiff prick with an audible plop, leaving my puckered rosette well lathered for the first time in its life. I had now lost my virginity with a vengeance.

Charles had now turned me on my back and we lay entwined on the sofa. He murmured that he hoped that I had enjoyed being bottom-fucked.

'At first it hurt somewhat, but then I must admit that the experience was most enjoyable.'

'There is a great advantage in bottom-fucking, Jenny,' he continued, 'and that is of course no lady can become *enceinte* and can enjoy as much cock as they desire without any worry of a swollen belly. You felt my cock throbbing away inside you just as if I were inside your cunt, did you not?'

'Yes,' I replied slowly, 'I cannot deny it. But I would prefer to keep my arsehole as an option to my cunney. How shall I put it, Charles? Perhaps by saying that if I am hungry for sexual sustenance, my cunney would be roast beef and my bumhole, Yorkshire pudding. If a choice were imposed, I could live happily on the meat and easily forgo the pudding.'

'Fair enough,' said Charles, 'yet I wager that as your bum becomes used to a cock sliding in and out between the cheeks, you will perforce have a change of heart and I hope that you will vary your diet accordingly.'

'Oh, I shall, dear Charles,' I giggled, 'after all, I have already done so today, have I not?'

'That you certainly have, Jenny, bless your little heart! Now just to show you that my tastes are eclectic, open your legs and let me fuck your pussey!'

'In a moment, Charles, we have plenty of time before the refreshment interval. In any case, you had better not exercise your darling prick too heavily as you did receive an awful blow to your bollocks out in the field.'

He looked at me and smiled broadly. 'If truth be told, I could easily have held the catch,' he admitted, 'but I let it appear that I was injured so I could pay courtship to you! Johnny had told me how much you enjoyed my acting last night. I hope I have proved to you how well I can perform in a private showing!'

I suppose that I should have been cross but frankly I had enjoyed myself and had felt honoured by his attention. I wish men would realize that, as the poet wrote, *Quae dant, quaeque negant gaudent tamen esse rogatae*! [Whether they give or refuse, women are glad to have been asked – Editor] Mind, men must also adhere to the corollary, in that they must respect the refusal of a girl, however quick the blood and however stiff the cock! Perhaps I have been fortunate for whenever I have found myself in a situation when a man wants to fuck me, if I have shown my wish to be left alone, this has been respected. I am careful, of course, in the choice of my companions and I have always refrained from what the vulgar classes know as 'prick-teasing'. A girl may show interest, kindness and affection but should not flirt with a man unless she is prepared to travel down the road to Journey's End.

And indeed, just then, I preferred to talk rather than fuck, and Charles, being a true gentleman, respected my wishes. I looked round at the fine paintings that adorned the study's walls.

'Charles, do you know anything about art? I am ignorant, I regert to say, but I know what paintings I like, and I do think that the portrait of a young man dressed in all the finery of a hundred years ago is most elegant. Do you know who the artist might be?'

'I'm not too well-up on the subject, my sweet, but I do happen to know a little about that painting. Lord Holne bought it last year from Sir Louis Segal, the textiles magnate. The painter was Brandl, if that means anything to you.'

'I'm afraid it does not, Charles. Is he still alive?'

'Oh, no, Brandl died in 1735. He was born in Prague and was a leading light in the Central European school of baroque art. He has an excellent feeling for the shape of the figure, has he not – and as Bertie Holne told me, and indeed this potted history of Brandl comes from his lips rather than mine, Brandl possessed an extraordinary talent for colour and light, for orchestrating contrasts of warm and cold shades.'

'I agree that he certainly creates a powerful influence upon the viewer,' I commented. 'Are his paintings expensive?'

'I believe Bertie had to fork out five hundred guineas and Sir Louis still grumbled that the work was worth even more.'

'Good heavens! All that money for a painting!'

'Yes, though ironically poor Brandl died in abject poverty. I fear that many artists are never appreciated during their own lifetimes.'

As I gazed at the portrait of a young man dressed in a brown velvet jacket, idly I tweaked one of my nipples which popped up like a little strawberry.

'Let me do that,' said Charles, caressing and cupping my full breasts with his hands. I began to breathe faster. My breasts were rising and falling, the nipples rosy-red with stiff delight as Charles continued to stroke them up to a peak of hardness.

'May I fuck your cunney now, please?' he asked.

I sighed my agreement and after a brief but passionate kiss, he pulled my legs apart to bury his face between them, licking and sucking at my damp pussey. He made appreciative little noises as he pleasured me, smacking his lips to let me know how much he was enjoying lapping up the flow of love-juice. His tongue stole into my slit, moving wetly up and down the furrow, gradually separating my cunt lips until the warm, rosy hole was exposed. He teased me by licking all round the spot, making me squirm and wriggle helplessly, my body shuddering with joy and frustration as I urged him to stick his clever tongue completely inside.

Charles tantalizingly darted his tongue all round my sopping sex lips, mixing his saliva with the lubricating juices that were now flowing from my cunt. My cunney lips were now drawn fully out by his teeth, and almost unbearable sensations seared through me as he nibbled on them. Then his tongue suddenly parted them, shoving deeply into my hole. My buttocks tensed as I teetered on the brink of spending; his nose nuzzled against my clitoris which was hard and erect, the tip standing clear of its hood. My pussey pushed hard against his face, and my hole convulsed around his tongue.

'Fuck me! Fuck me!' I cried out desperately. My wet, open cunt now frantically needed a throbbing, stiff cock to fill it and complete my ecstacy.

So ever the gentleman, Charles raised himself up and taking his long rammer in his hand, directed the swollen dome directly at the portals of my yearning cunney. Well moistened as I was, his long shaft eased into me as if oiled. Our bellies touched as he squeezed every last inch of his divine cock between the waiting walls of my willing notch, stretching and gorging it to the fullest extent. As his pelvis jabbed down, I eagerly lifted my hips to welcome his driving tool that slid squelchily in and out of my cunt. I lifted my bum, rotating wildly to achieve the maximum contact and as I twisted and turned in the delights of my overwhelming spend, Charles emptied himself into my dripping pit.

We enjoyed yet a third jousting which perhaps over-exhausted us for we lay insensible whilst the teams trooped off the field for the tea-break.

I awoke first to find myself clutching Charles' semi-erect cock. I had a mind to take matters further so I kissed his eyes, nose and mouth which broke his slumber most deliciously and turned him over to lie on his back, pushing a cushion under his hips so that his slim, manly buttocks were lifted towards me. I caressed his bum and slipped my hand into the crevice between his cheeks. Now it was my turn to use my tongue, licking the so-sensitive perineum, the small area between his balls and arsehole. I moistened the mobile tip of my tongue making the place slippery with my saliva until Charles could stand the exquisite sensation no longer.

He rolled over onto his back and I leaped up on him, seizing the iron shaft in my hands and rubbing it in my cleft, rubbing it there in that wet, warm place, resisting the temptation to insert the ruby uncapped head until I felt ready to receive it. When I judged that my pussey was ready to entertain this welcome guest, I pushed down, steering the plump head between the lips of my cunt. I pushed again and again bouncing up and down, quickening my tempo, feeling more joy with each thrust.

The pulsing in my pussey increased to a new quickness as the welcome warmth of Charles' ever ready charger plunged into my willing cunt, drenching my womb with a perfect shower of spunk.

We joyously screamed out our climaxes when to my horror, I saw Johnny standing just a few feet away together with a handsome young boy from Lord Holne's team between whose white-flannelled legs stood out such an enormous bulge that his cock must have been fairly bursting.

'Is this how you carry on as soon as my back is turned?' said Johnny with mock severity. 'And is this a sight for young Richard Russell who has only just attained his sixteenth birthday and has probably never seen a naked girl in the flesh before now?'

Charles looked somewhat embarrassed but I cared not a fig – after all, had not Johnny arranged for his friend to share my favours? I might as well enjoy the situation to the full, I thought, so I shrugged my shoulders and said: 'Richard has never seen the undraped female form? Is that true, my bright young spark?'

Richard was a good-looking, blond-haired boy with delicate features, although he was shortly to prove that his body was indeed masculine!

I repeated my question. 'Is it true then that I am the first girl you have ever seen in the nude?'

He was still a little tongue-tied but he nodded his assent.

'Well, then, it must follow that the only intercourse you have enjoyed is in your imagination. You must have dreamed many times about having a fuck,' I said decisively, 'and I am certain that you would not be averse to having one now.'

Richard remained silent but his eyes sparkled and Charles grinned: 'He would rather have a fuck than score a century for England at Lord's, wouldn't you, young shaver?'

This time Richard spoke up in a clear, boyish voice. 'I would like nothing better,' he said simply, 'except that I am not expert and –'

'You mean you are a virgin,' interrupted Johnny. 'Well, we all were virgins once and it is in no way a disgrace. You do toss off, though, don't you?'

The boy blushed and nodded his head: 'Well, yes, I mean

we all do at school. But I'm sure there is a great difference between imitation and the genuine article.'

'Of course there is,' I said warmly, 'but I don't think we will experience any great difficulty if that bulge in your trousers is anything to go by!'

Without further ado, I quickly pulled Richard closer. I was now sitting down on the sofa and Charles moved over so that Richard could sit down next to me. Johnny bent down and sitting on the floor, removed Richard's cricket shoes and socks. I began undoing the buttons of his shirt and Charles eased the boy's head between my ample bare breasts. He may have been a virgin but he knew what to do next! He soon fastened his mouth over one of my nipples, sucking gently at the tip till it shot up stiff with excitement. I now craved for more than having my titties sucked so I told the sweet lad to stand up whilst Johnny unbuttoned his trousers and Charles pulled down his drawers. His handsome young prick stood stiffly to attention as I gently pushed him back upon the couch. I kissed his lips and he responded with unbridled lust, opening his mouth for my tongue to dart between his teeth. I squeezed his youthful body hard against mine as his young cock twitched uncontrollably as I grasped his stiff shaft and peeled back the foreskin with one hand and fondled his small balls with the other.

As might have been expected, the first touch of a soft, feminine hand on his stiff cock was too much to bear, and he whimpered with frustration as his body went rigid and a creamy emission of frothy white sperm shot out of his knob like a miniature fountain, drenching the cushion, alas, although as I now know, Peggy Popper's Household Cleaning Liquid is most efficacious at removing spunk stains.

However, Richard's cock was still heavy with desire so I lightly frigged his shaft, playing with his foreskin, capping and uncapping the purplish red knob that I knew would soon be ready for its maiden voyage.

'Are you ready, Richard?' I asked. 'There is no hurry, do take your time.'

'I am quite ready, Miss Jenny. Oh, please let me put my prick inside you!' he begged.

I lay on my back, opened my legs to afford the boy a good look at his first cunney and held his cock as he clambered on top of me. I let the knob rub against my bushy mound for a moment and then I eased the virgin tool inside, spreading my legs well apart to enable him to push further down. Once he was well inside, I wrapped my legs around his body and urged him to begin fucking. Nothing loath, he began to push forwards and backwards and what the boy lacked in experience he made up for with enthusiasm. His jerking became even faster as he plunged deeper and deeper, his cock delighting in this first experience of being caressed by the slippery membranes of a real cunt instead of the usual four fingered widow!

All of this action was meat and drink to Charles and Johnny. Johnny had divested himself of his clothes and so like Charles stood absolutely naked, watching with fascination as Richard pumped merrily away. His first spunking caused by the excitement of my hand on his shaft enabled him to fuck with increasing vigour without spending.

I urged my young sport to pace himself and to slow down his strokes. 'As in playing cricket, timing is all important. Slowly now as I cannot come as quickly as you,' I instructed, as Charles and Johnny kneeled down so I could suck one prick whilst tossing off the other one.

Now Richard's *coup de grâce* was fast approaching, which I could tell from the manner of his fast breathing and throbbing cock. I stopped sucking Johnny's prick but grasped hold of it with my hand so that I was tossing off Johnny with my left hand and Charles with my right.

My cunt thrust upwards in one last effort to cram even more of that magic stiffness inside me as his balls banged against my arse. I tensed to receive his wodge as his cock jerked wildly inside me and he shot his first wodge of creamy jism into me as torrents of my own juices mingled happily with his as I reached the crest of delight.

Almost simultaneously the two cocks I was masturbating shot their loads, sending streams of white froth cascading across my titties. Oh, the lewdness of it all! But I did enjoy it so!

It was as well that Johnny had possessed the foresight to lock the study door as we had only a short time to clean ourselves up with the towels Charles had thoughtfully borrowed from one of the dressing-rooms. We were startled by a loud thump on the door and the fruity voice of our genial host was heard: 'I say, you chaps, time to get back to the fray, what!'

'We won't be but a minute, Bertie,' Charles called back, 'just half a jiffy and we will be with you.'

Johnny's team was now batting and this enabled him to sit with us. In any case, Charles told Lord Holne that he was now fully recovered so both my beaus were able to dance attendance upon me. It was deemed best for all concerned that young Richard stayed with his team-mates. The lad's first fuck obviously inspired the young scamp as he was now at the crease and knocking the bowling all over the shop.

I have no great opinions about our national summer sport – cricket, I mean, not fucking – but Charles and Johnny engaged in a heated argument about whether the quality of the game had declined in recent years.

Charles was quite positive that the quality of bowling had deteriorated. 'For a start, there are no fast bowlers left of the speed of Sayers, Waller or Caughey,' he declared, 'and our present medium-pace men have nearly all adopted the "over-shoulder" system. This system, while giving the bowler greater accuracy regarding straightness, diminishes the chance of getting a wicket,'he said heatedly.

I feigned interest for the sake of politeness. 'Why is that so?' I said.

'Because the natural method of delivering a ball is in a line nearly level with the shoulder. Some years ago, Edgar Willsher was almost the only man who raised his arm higher than that point. Now it seems that all bowlers are copying his action,' Charles continued.

'Ah, this may be so,' said Johnny, 'but the "over-shoulder" man may gain in precision.'

'I do not agree,' said Charles, 'I can remember bowlers of the old school bowling maiden after maiden in succession. And do you not remember old Billy Caffyn amusing the spectators by bowling into a cap placed on the ground between the wickets? Let us face it, how many single stumps have gone flying, seen bowled out of the ground?

'I have been to several matches this season and have only seen two take a walk – one sent flying by Bowley at the Oval and the other by young Pilch at Lord's,' he added.

This conversation went on for about half an hour but I did not concern myself to listen in earnest. I was far more concerned with applauding my supple young lover who celebrated the loss of his virginity by almost single-handedly winning the game for his side by carrying his bat for a splendid one hundred and twelve runs, not out!

We cheered Richard and all the players off the field and enjoyed a refreshing cup of tea and a fine variety of light refreshments before thanking Lord Holne for his hospitality. We gave Charles a lift back to the Adelphi and decided to dine at the Argyle Rooms with Harold Le Meshigunah who was back in town, and Johnny thought it prudent to accept his brother-in-law's invitation. 'He will be only too pleased if you come with me, Jenny,' said Johnny. 'With luck you will keep him sweet and the old beggar will keep the boodle coming my way!'

I changed into a fetching gold coloured frock, low cut with a cascade of lace that just covered enough of my bosom for decency yet somehow accentuated the ripe contours of my breasts.

Johnny went home to change into evening dress and returned in a hansom as, not unreasonably, Monsieur Le

Meshigunah wanted his carriage for his own use. Aunt Portia had not returned from her meeting so I left a note with the servants to say where Johnny and I were dining and that she should not trouble to wait up for me.

'Are we going into the heart of our capital?' I asked Johnny as we journeyed to our destination.

'Rather,' he replied. 'The Argyle Rooms are just off the Haymarket. It used to be a public house but is now the finest casino in London. Actually, we shall be dining at some rather expensive club privee to which Harold belongs. I must warn you, Jenny, that Harold fancies himself as a cocksman and I would not be surprised if there were at least one young lady besides yourself dining at our table tonight.'

'Goodness me, you don't mean that Harold consorts with prostitutes,' I exclaimed.

'I regret to say that he does just that,' said Johnny, 'and I suppose you are now going to tell me that I should inform his wife, my eldest sister, Ada, all about his nocturnal affairs.'

'No, that did not occur to me although now you mention it, I suppose that many would feel their duty to so do.'

'Well, I have thought about it but then I have always believed in the old saying that none should interfere between husband and wife. Perhaps Ada does not enjoy the delights of *l'arte de faire l'amour*. Perhaps she prefers that Harold takes his pleasures away from the marriage bed. Perhaps she too has a lover – no, don't look so shocked, my dear Jenny, a goodly number of married women have been known to partake of forbidden fruit. So all in all, I have so far judged it best not to mention a word to anyone about this matter except you, and that is only because I know you to be liberally minded and can, if need be, keep a secret.'

'Yet you feel no compunction accepting Harold's hospitality or his augmenting your allowance?'

'Why not? He has plenty to spare so why not keep it in the family?'

I was not entirely convinced of Johnny's logic but allowed myself to be temporarily persuaded at least for the time being. I would reserve judgement, I decided, until I met Monsieur Le Meshigunah for myself.

I enjoyed the ride through the grand streets of the West End of London and marvelled at the numbers of the crowds that jostled along the pavements.

Perhaps no sight makes a more profund impression on the mind of the stranger than the brilliant gaiety of Regent Street and its environs. It is not only the architectural splendour of the aristocratic streets in that neighbourhood but the brilliant illumination of the shops, cafés and concert rooms, and the troops of elegantly dressed, fashionable women rustling in silks and satins escorted by the high bred gentlemen of fashion and scions of the aristocracy. Yet the street contains persons of all classes, of every order and pursuit, from the ragged crossing sweeper and tattered shoe-black to the hordes of ladies of pleasure.

'There appear to be an extraordinary number of girls walking the streets,' I said in all innocence.

Johnny gave a short laugh and said: 'Oh, yes, Jenny, there are always many street walkers around this area. Why, you silly goose, most of those girls, dressed though they may be in the height of fashion, are ladies of the night, looking for gallants.'

'There must be great competition. I have never seen so many girls and many look quite young and attractive.'

'Many of them are earning as much as thirty pounds a week on their backs but it is not an occupation I would recommend.'

'A pity there is no call for the services of boys or you would be able to dispense with the generosity of Harold Le Meshigunah!'

'There is such a demand but as it comes from other men, I'll be buggered if I'll do it!'

'Well, that's true enough!' I said quickly and we both roared with laughter as the hansom stopped outside a house in Queen Street in close proximity to the Argyle Rooms.

'Here we are, Jenny, this is where we will dine,' said Johnny.

'I did not know we were invited to a private house. I thought you said we were going across the road to the Argyle Rooms.'

'Later in the evening we shall play roulette there, my love. But in any case, this is not a private residence as such. It is a house owned by the Jim-Jam Club, a very select group of wealthy men who enjoy fast but discreet pleasures. Harold is a country member and that sets him back three hundred pounds a year. In addition, all expenses he incurs have to be settled within a month of their being incurred or the member is expelled.

'There are so many would-be members that bills are settled very promptly even though a bottle of champagne costs seventeen shillings and sixpence, which is at least double what you would expect to pay, and an evening at the Jim-Jam may cost up to as much as five pounds! And that does not include any present you may be forced to give to a girl who has consented to be your bed-fellow for the night.

'I am sure that Harold has asked us to meet him here because he has made an assignment with a damsel who is no better than she should be,' he added.

We entered the establishment after Johnny had presented his card to the hulking major domo who, checking a list of names written on a sheet of paper taken from his pocket, escorted us without comment into a richly-furnished drawing-room'

'I shouldn't think that the Club will be crowded until later on,' said Johnny, 'as tonight there is a new production at the Alhambra and every member worth his salt wishes to fuck Mrs Dolly Delamere, the leading lady. That is the case, is it not, Dodds?'

'Very true, sir,' assented the big servant, 'and the staff are laying seven to four on Lord Skinner being first in her, though Colonel Tucker swears he will spare no expense to have the lady in question suck his cock.'

'I would not bet against Lord Skinner who is a most determined chap, Dodds, so put me down for a tenner on his victory.'

'I am very sorry, sir,' said Dodds, 'the book is for members only. Meanwhile, may I suggest a glass of wine for yourself and your guest? Monsieur Le Meshigunah will be with you shortly.'

'Do you know when he is arriving?' I asked.

'He is already here, ma'am, but is upstairs in one of the upper chambers with the fourth member of your dinner party,' Dodds said solemnly.

'Good heavens, what a randy old goat! Jenny, that is where the fucking takes place,' said Johnny with a flash of annoyance. 'I do think he might have had the courtesy to wait until after we had dined. I don't know about you but I'm devilish hungry and I don't want to wait too long to feed my face.'

As it happens, we had only time to sip our champagne before our host appeared. Harold was a dark, good-looking man of some thirty-five years of age, quite tall and well-built although his saturnine features were evidence of his being born under a brighter sun than that which hovers over this sceptred isle.

Clutching his arm was a most beautiful girl of about twenty-three, and I was not over-pleased that Johnny licked his lips whilst the introductions were made.

The girl's name was Kate and she was attired in a simple yet elegant pink gown which like mine was cut as low as possible without shocking, only half concealing a pair of ripe globes, whilst her waist was as slender as a nymph's. To complete my discomfort, I must record her pretty features, a small mouth inlaid with two rows of ivory, lips rosy and pouting, cheeks soft as the velvet down of an overripe peach, languishing dark eyes, sparkling and beaming with a lascivious fire, shaded by silken lashes, whilst her auburn hair fell in a profusion of ringlets over her neck and shoulders.

'Have you and Kate known each other long, Harold?' asked Johnny.

'No, not really,' said Harold in his not unattractive foreign accent. 'We met this afternoon in Burlington Arcade. I was walking from Sackville Street where Mr Rabinowitz had given me a second fitting for my new smoking jacket when we bumped into each other as I think the saying goes.'

'Well, we do have an acquaintance in common, don't we?' said Kate.

'You mean old Simeon Scott?' said Harold. 'Yes, yes, I'm surprised an old roué like Simeon is still out on the town. He must be sixty if he's a day, and Dodds tells me that ten years ago he won the Jim-Jam's monthly Victor Pudendum Trophy five times in a row and took second place three times.'

'Last year he was mentioned in despatches so to speak,' said Johnny, 'I just don't know how he keeps it up.'

'That's just what he can do so well,' laughed Kate. 'I've never known a gentleman who can keep his cock stiff so long without spending his sperm.'

They explained to me that this keenly fought-for honour consisted of a monthly fucking competition. Entrants had to fuck before a panel of judges who awarded marks for style, grace, novelty and ingenuity, so it was far removed from those silly tossing-off competitions in which young boys indulge. There the winner is the one who can spurt furthest or quickest.

But the Victor Pudendum was a far more sophisticated affair. Betting was allowed with Dodds making the book and all profits being donated to the Society for the Spreading Of Useful Information which distributed tracts on birth control to the ignorant masses.

Entrants were restricted to members of the Jim-Jam and their guests whilst the girls were cocottes from the very highest ranks. It costs one hundred guineas to enter plus a fee of twenty-five pounds for the services of the partner. The winning pair each receive a gift, the member getting a gold cup and the girl one hundred sovereigns.

Eminent men about town such as Lord Norrogh, Harknett Dixon and Sir Lionel Trapes acted as judges with Doctor Jonathan Arkley often acting as the official adjudicator.

'When is the next contest?' I asked.

'Why, Jenny, surely you would not wish to enter!' said Johnny.

'No, but I would love to watch as I am sure I would learn some worthwhile accomplishments,' I replied.

'We only have room for a limited audience,' said Harold, 'and tickets are fifty pounds each and are in great demand. HRH never misses a Victor Pudendum if he can help it. Still, I will see what I can do.'

In the splendid dining room we enjoyed a most superb dinner. There was little conversation as the food and drink were so admirable and the service so perfect that we concentrated solely upon assuaging our hunger and thirst.

We began with caviare followed by Sole Au Vin Blanc (it was too warm an evening for soup) and Poulet a l'Indien all washed down with Veuve Clicquot, 1864. We sipped coffee together as neither man wished to partake of the Club's 1858 Cognac.

'Now if we are all ready, let us repair to the casino,' said Harold. 'I feel lucky tonight and that my name will be amongst the winners.'

So we strolled over to the Argyle Rooms and talking of nomenclatures, I asked Harold the derivation of his unusual name, saying that I hoped my question did not offend.

'No, Jenny, of course not,' said Harold. 'As Johnny may have told you, my mother is Belgian but my father hailed from Bohemia.

'His family served Count Svitavou who owned the famous Rajac chateau, the best Louis XVI style chateau in South

Moravia. Perhaps you know it? No? Well, it is fine example of baroque architecture of three wings surrounding a courtyard.

'The central building features a representative storey, private accommodation quarters and an entresol reserved for servants. The façades of the chateau are coloured in different shades.

'One of the most valuable rooms is the picture gallery which contains mostly French and German works of Romanticism along with some seventeenth century Dutch paintings.'

'Is there a Brandl there?' I asked.

'You know of Brandl, my dear. You are well informed indeed. No, and I would dearly like to lay my hands on a Brandl portrait. Sir Louis Segal laid his hands on one but I believe he sold it.'

'Yes, to Lord Holne,' said Johnny, 'we saw it there this afternoon in his study.'

'Thank you for the information. I must ask Bertie Holne if he will countenance an offer. Anyhow, to return to your question, my dear Jenny, my father Max Le Meshigunah shot a mad dog that was about to attack the Count's youngest son. The nobleman was so grateful that he gave my father a generous gift and my father used the money wisely and travelled around Europe. He met my mother, whose aunt is the Marquise de Bruxelles, and their love-match produced me!

'My father set up a publishing house in his adopted country but he always had a great admiration for the British so he insisted I learned English and completed my education at Oxford University.'

'That is very interesting, Harold,' I said. 'And does your education extend to teaching me how to play roulette?'

'The pleasure will be mine,' said Harold gallantly.

'I hope not,' muttered Johnny, 'she has had more than her fair share of cock today and mine will be the only prick entering her pussey tonight!'

I ignored his coarse remark which perhaps fortunately Harold did not hear. Harold explained the rules of roulette to me. I sat next to Harold and staked exactly as he did though with not such high stakes. The consequence was that I won twenty-eight pounds and I shall treat myself to a new outfit!

Kate had also won a small amount at the roulette table although Johnny had not encountered good fortune and was some ten pounds lighter in pocket.

We strolled back to the Jim-Jam where the impassive Dodds led us through to Harold's suite of rooms.

'Would you excuse us for a while, ladies,' said Harold, 'as Johnny and I have some business to discuss. We will be some thirty minutes. Meanwhile, would you like Dodds to bring up some drinks?'

'A bottle of champagne is always pleasant to have at hand,' said Kate.

'Very good, my dear. Dodds, a bottle of the house champagne, please. Ladies, Johnny and I will see you later,' he said, closing the door.

Dodds returned a couple of minutes later with a silver tray on which there were two glasses and a bottle of champagne in an ice-bucket.

'Thank you,' said Kate, turning to me. 'Jenny, shall we open this now or wait a while.'

'I think I would prefer to wait,' I said. 'My goodness, it is so damnably hot this evening. I enjoy the sunshine but in the evening I do find this intense heat somewhat oppressive especially in town.'

'So do I, my dear,' she rejoined, 'so much so in fact that I am going to take off all my clothes!'

She slipped out of her dress and let it fall to the floor. Then, she sat down on the sofa and peeled off her stockings and she looked at me in a knowing and confident way.

'Are you not hot, Jenny?' she asked. 'Why do you not follow my example.'

She stood up and undid her corsets, letting free two

magnificent large breasts tipped with large strawberry nipples that just asked to be taken in my mouth, which positively watered at the thought.

In a trice, I quickly disrobed and Kate took a few steps towards me, planted her hands on the sides of my face and gently kissed me on the mouth. She kissed me again and looked at me, smiling . . . and then it was I who kissed her. My arms went up around her neck and I clung to her that way for some time, our mouths glued together and our tongues playing back and forth in each other's mouths.

I let go of her and took a step backwards. Kate was completely naked and her body was one of the most beautiful I had ever seen or imagined. She was tall, with a slender figure, yet possesses these large yet firm, uptilted breasts, a flat belly, narrow waist and long tapering legs between which nestled a thickly curled thatch of auburn moss.

Kate took my hand and led me into the bedroom. I held back only an instant in the doorway but my blood was up and I made no resistance as she laid me down upon the wide bed. A moment later I felt Kate's mouth and tongue start a grand tour of my body, touching, kissing, lapping every inch of me until her tongue sank itself between my cunney lips.

'Oh, Kate, that's quite lovely. Oh, more! More! More!' I panted, as my bottom jerked upwards as Kate's clever little tongue wriggled between my pussey, driving it right inside my cunt, tossing it around the juicy walls of my vagina, withdrew it then plunged it in deeply. Up and down, in and out did her long tongue lap up my slippery juices as I threw my legs high up upon her shoulders. A girl's tongue is ever more delicate and somehow more knowing than a man's and I was already trembling at the very gate of Paradise.

'Jenny! Jenny! What a delicious slit you have!' she gasped, wrenching her mouth from my trembling cunt and replacing it with her fingers. 'How quickly your nipples come up. May I suck them?'

'Heavens, yes!' I assented and within a mere two or three

minutes, with the quivering buds of my nipples now quite erect through the ministrations of Kate's craftily sucking mouth and my thighs twisting to capture her wrist as she continued to push two fingers in and out of my now dripping cunt, I could feel the rushing approach of heavenly bliss.

As I felt the imminent orgasm swell up inside me, I hauled Kate into my arms and crushed those soft breasts hard against mine as we kissed again, feverishly and lasciviously, until the eruption inside me made me arch back, crying out once more as the storm shook my body to ruins.

Kate did not have to say a word to me for I knew that now I should do to her what she had done so expertly to me.

My hands ran gently over her body as I lowered myself upon her and began to suck those delicious red nipples which stood up like stalks as I licked and sucked upon them. I stroked the silky auburn notch of cunney hair and I tingled all over as the ripe wet lips of her cunt opened under my probing. The skin of her pussey was gorgeously soft and moist and I slid my fingers effortlessly inside her cunt.

Now I frigged slowly into her, slithering my lips gradually downwards until they were directly over her cunt. Meanwhile, Kate wriggled her body across so she could slip herself across the bed in a ninety degree turn. My mouth never left her juicy pussey as she, now with her head directly under my cunt, grasped my thighs and brought my own dripping muff down upon her eager mouth. We sighed and groaned together as we now lay side by side with our heads deep between each other's legs. I was tonguing deep inside of this pretty young girl and her juices were running and her clitty was enormous with excitement. I nipped her clitty, playfully sucking and biting it as her hands clasped my swinging titties as she greedily sucked up the juices that were pouring from my pussey, titillating and lapping in such a rapturous manner that her face was almost drowned by my copious emission as I went off into a most delicious state of almost unconscious lethargy.

After we had composed ourselves, Kate padded across the room to fetch in the champagne. She popped the cork and poured the sparkling wine into two glasses. She handed me one and lifted hers to propose a toast.

'What shall we drink to?' she inquired with a saucy grin.

'How about to our cunnies,' I laughed. 'May they never dry up and continue to receive as many mouths, fingers and cocks as we desire.'

'Yes, indeed,' said Kate. 'I did so enjoy making love with you, Jenny, and the embrace of a pretty girl is an important part of my intimate desires. But equally important is a good thick prick as I am sure you will agree.'

'I could not agree with you more, Kate,' I said. 'I do love stroking cocks, kissing and sucking them and of course to have one fuck my cunt.'

'Yes, it takes an awful lot to beat a fine upstanding prick,' said Kate. 'Yet you know, Jenny, some men are very foolish about their equipment. They imagine their cocks to be too small.'

'Do they really, Kate?'

'Yes, so many boys consider the size of their cocks to be inadequate but in truth they have no problem at all. Now I do not deny that a slightly thicker tool does make me lick my lips but five inches, for example, is more than adequate.

'I have seen many pricks and I can assure you that an eight or nine inch organ is very rare. The majority of the male population share the same sized pricks and I am sure you will agree with me that it is not the size of the cock that counts but more the ability any man may have to satisfy a girl through his own mastery of the technique of fucking.

'After all, fucking is an art and if carried out with style and panache with no thought about size, I am sure that more men would enjoy better sex lives!' she concluded.

I changed the direction of the conversation and asked Kate if I could ask her a delicate question.

'Of course you may, Jenny,' she answered, 'though I am certain I already know the nature of your query. You would like to ascertain how I feel taking money for letting men fuck me. I am right, am I not?'

'Yes, Kate,' I said, somewhat abashedly, 'I hope you do not think my inquiry somewhat rude.'

'Not at all,' she replied gaily, 'you would be far from the first person to ask me that same question.

'The truth is, Jenny, that I was born in Camberley where my father owned a small draper's shop. Life there was terribly dull and I thought that there had to be a more interesting life than minding the shop occasionally or attending to some minor domestic matter. I had no occasion to mix with members of the opposite sex although at night my cunney burned for the touch of a good prick. I had no idea what a stiff cock looked like at this time, of course, as the only pricks I had ever seen were little boys' doodles at school.

'Well, for my seventeenth birthday, my parents decided to take me to London to the theatre, which I admit was most kind of them. I remember my father saying to my mother, "There is something good at the Haymarket, according to the newspaper, The Merry Wives of Windsor."

'"It is Shakespeare, Philip," said my mother, peering over his shoulder, and that settled the question. We sat in the dress circle. Shakespeare or no, it was too outspoken a comedy for a girl of seventeen. I was now determined to go to London and seek my fortune on the stage. I was able to play the piano tolerably well and have a naturally fair singing voice.

'But I did not wish to make the pilgrimage to London by myself so I chose to take with me young Roger, the handsome boy who was apprenticed to my father. He was the same age as myself and I knew that he would follow me anywhere if there was the remotest chance of his having his way with me. I had no objection to that but had not allowed him the slightest liberty until now as I knew that I should not part with this ace until I could obtain something worthwhile for it.

'So that night, after my parents had gone to bed, I stole up to the attic to Roger's bedroom. I had not been overhead and I put my eye to the keyhole to see if the young spark was asleep.

'Jenny, I was truly amazed at what I saw! There was Roger, lying naked on the bed holding a magazine in his left hand and with his right hand he was massaging this great swollen shaft between his legs. Oh, but he looked so sweet as I gazed upon his manly torso with wonder and admiration. He looked so lithe and handsome but naturally it was his stiff grand-looking prick and his big balls in their handsome bags that most attracted my eyes.

'I gazed in awe of this velvet-skinned rod which stood so proudly to attention as he stroked back what I now know to be the foreskin to allow full view of the purple-domed knob. I felt a moistness between my own thighs and pulling up my nightdress, I began to finger my cunney. But I knew I wanted more than my own fingers between my legs and so I gave my ample bush a final stroke and boldly opened the door. Goodness, you should have seen Roger's face. All the colour drained out of his cheeks in an instant! "My God! Miss Kate! What are you doing here? Oh! Oh! I shall lose my position!" he gasped.

'"The only position you will lose is the present one which is with your lovely cock at half-mast!" I said smoothly, shutting the door behind me and taking the wise precaution of turning the key which was an action Roger had singularly failed to perform. He just lay there gasping at first with fright and then with wonderment as I opened the buttons of my nightdress and pulled it up and over the top of my head giving the boy what must have been his first view of the naked female form.

'I did not bother with any preliminaries but reached for his cock which was not erect but still thick with unslaked passion. It sprang to life in my hand, thickening and swelling to its previously proud high state. Roger's cock was one of the thickest if not the longest I have ever grasped as I could barely close my fingers around it. Slowly at first, I ran my hand up and down the length, then I tightened my grip and began to jerk him. It was all so natural, somehow I just knew what to do even though I had never held a cock in my hand before. I delicately encircled the bulbous head and lowered my head to implant a kiss upon it. This excited Roger even more and I had only licked this mushroom once when his prick began to twitch uncontrollably as this strange white froth came bubbling out of his knob. I jammed my mouth over the dome and slurped up the cream which I found most pleasant to taste. I gulped and sucked every drop until his cock shrank back to its normal size.

'Now it was Roger's turn to explore my body. "Oh, Kate," he said, his voice throbbing with emotion, "I have dreamed so often of fucking you. You are such a beautiful girl and your titties, God your titties . . ." His voice trailed off as I gently pulled him towards me and I took his hand and encouraged him to roll my nipple until it was as hard as a pebble.

'He kissed my neck and throat and then moved down to my breasts and sucked hard on my engorged nipples. I pulled his head down towards my bush and he sucked greedily over my pouting cunney-lips and without bringing me off by sucking my cunney – he was far too eager to insert his cock, which was understandable in the circumstances – he brought the head of his cock to my eager pussey.

'So I took hold of this throbbing monster and guided it with my own hands to its haven. The sensation of his warm, thick prick squeezing into my virgin quimmy made me groan with desire and excitement. My whole body began to tingle and soon I was coming off in a series of delirious spendings. All too soon he began to shudder and he held me in a really tight grip as we shuddered to a glorious mutual climax. I shall never forget that first fuck, short as it was; and the loss of my virginity afforded little pain.

'The sperm that Roger spilled into my cunt had penetrated and further oiled the dark passage so my hymen was ruptured without much difficulty as his fierce lunges pushed the head of his cock deeper and deeper inside me. The final cunney-rending thrust led to his burying the length of that thick shaft up to the hilt and his big hairy balls banged against my bum. The shock added to the piquancy of the moment and I revelled in his delightful cock enveloping itself within the soft, luscious folds of my love sheath.

'When we had recovered from our delirium, I told him that he now had to leave my father's employ or I would tell Papa that he had forced his unwanted desires upon me. I had not needed to utter the threat as Roger was more than eager for an adventure especially if more pussey would be made available to him. So the very next night we left the house with just a few pounds of our joint savings between us. I would not rob my parents and indeed still occasionally send money back home to them as often as I can.

'We soon tired of each other as you may have expected and I was as eager to leave Roger as he was to leave me. Only a few days afterwards, I dressed up in my finest clothes, and walked through the Haymarket to take coffee at Sam's Cafe. By sheer chance, I literally bumped into Sir Bolton Glasgow who at first sight became enamoured and after a little preliminary conversation, we retired to Sir Bolton's chambers in Golden Square where without even asking for prior reward I unbuttoned his trousers, released his bursting cock and gobbled his throbbing tool as if it were a sweetmeat.

'Sir Bolton wanted to fuck me then and there but I would not allow him to do that until I had explained my lonely and somewhat worrisome pecuniary state. "Never mind about that, Kate," cried the randy baronet, "I will set you up in a fine house I own in Mount Street and there I will mount you at least three times a day!"

'He was as good as his word and allowed me a most generous amount of money and I lived in excellent style. He came to the house as often as he could and we fucked very often. But poor Sir Bolton suffered greatly from a premature spurting of his seed and I found the fucking frustrating rather than an enjoyable experience. I began to yearn for a lover who could better satisfy my body and I took up with Sir Bolton's nephew, the Hon. Bradley Clive. Alas, I was indiscreet and one of Sir Bolton's servants who waited upon me decided to sneak after I had reprimanded her over a badly prepared breakfast. That afternoon, Sir Bolton gave me my freedom and took away the housekeys, giving me twenty-four hours to pack up my belongings and find a new home.

'I was forced to pawn most of his presents of jewellery but I soon met other gallant young gentlemen and set myself up in my own small yet quite luxurious home off the Tottenham Court Road. I have enjoyed the discreet company of two wealthy gentlemen, Sir Preston Pinner and Captain Clarke of the 69th Lancers, but both are now away and so I sauntered down to the Burlington Arcade this afternoon where I met Harold. I shall let him fuck me if he pays well as I do not wish to dip into my bank account.'

'But Kate, do you not want to settle down and marry?' I said.

'Oh, yes, in good time,' she replied, 'and you must remember that I enjoy my life. I have all I want and my gentlemen love me to excess. Of course my parents do not know what I am doing although if they had any real thoughts on the matter they might guess that I am earning my bread lying on my back! But as for marriage – I could marry tomorrow if I liked.'

I later learned that this attitude was common amongst ladies of the town and the next day when I related this conversation to Johnny he told me that I should treat the tale "with a pinch of salt". I dare say he is probably right.

'These women live entirely for the moment,' he commented, 'and they care little about the morrow until pressed in any way and then they are fertile in expedients to justify their mode of existence.'

I am tired of writing now although I have not yet finished the story of that first night at the Jim-Jam Club. I shall continue the tale frankly without embellishment or omission tomorrow, diary, as I bid you good night.

August 10th, 1871

I know I am falling behind recording the events of these last few hectic days. So I am determined to spend the entire day in my room putting pen to paper and bringing you up to date, dear diary, with what has been going on. Tomorrow we leave for Scotland and The Glorious Twelfth so I promise that today I shall spend every moment, diary, in your company.

(The next two months were to be quite extraordinary even in the crowded life of Jenny Everleigh and will be published complete in the next book, Volume Five, of this series – Editor).

So to reset the scene, Kate and I were lying nude on the bed, sipping champagne whilst she told me of her present lifestyle and how she came by it.

The champagne had the effect of revitalizing us and soon we were kissing and cuddling again in the old lascivious fashion when our reverie was suddenly interrupted. We were so busy sucking out each other's pussies that we had not heard Harold and Johnny's return.

'Ah ha, what have we here, John?' exclaimed Harold. 'It looks to me as if these ladies prefer dildoes to pricks.'

Kate disentangled her mouth from my groin and coolly replied: 'Well you two have been so long that we had to start without you.'

'We are only a little late,' said Johnny, 'and we would have returned before only we met Professor Potts the phrenologist who insisted on examining Harold's bumps.'

I said that I knew little of phrenology except that my Uncle Walter owned an old book entitled *The Constitution of Man* by George Combe.

'He was one of the founders of the science,' said Harold. 'Why he even read the bumps of the President of America and our own dear Queen's children, Albert and Alice, when they were very small.'

'What did Professor Potts say of your head?' asked Kate, slipping her hand across to unbutton Harold's trousers.

'It was most interesting. He said I had good bumps of aspiration, especially of firmness and conscientiousness but poor bumps of tune and colour. My largest bumps were those of combativeness and acquisitiveness, which I suppose must be right as I do enjoy my work and always want to expand my affairs.'

'You are doing very well in expanding your affairs,' smiled Kate, bringing Harold's thickening prick out of the bursting confines of his trousers.

'I am sure that Jenny and I could feel your bumps to better effect than that displayed even by the great Professor Potts,' said Kate decisively, slowly frigging Harold's swollen prick that twitched and jerked away as she capped and uncapped the vermilion head that seemed to grow even larger under her gentle touch.

I wriggled to the other side of the bed and beckoned Johnny to come and sit with me as I knew that the preliminary jousting between Kate and Harold would very soon lead to a fully blown fuck and I also knew that I wanted to watch it all happen!

Kate pulled Harold by his prick to sit down on the bed and, still holding his stiff shaft in her right hand, parted her legs wide and sensuously stroked the insides of her thighs with her delicate fingers.

'Ah, Kate, my precious, you are exciting me beyond belief,' croaked Harold. 'Here let me help you . . .' and he leaned across to stroke the auburn muff between her legs like a cat lover with his favourite Persian whilst Kate let go his jutting prick and began to unbutton his shirt. It took but a minute for Harold to kick and tug off his clothes and now they both lay nude on the bed, kissing passionately with

Kate rubbing Harold's prick up to a stupendous flagpole of hardness and Harold repaying the compliment by sucking and slurping away on one enlarged tawny nipple and flicking and rubbing the other up to equal height with the palm of his hand. Harold was now on top of her and to help matters along I slid across the bed on my hands and knees to take hold of Harold's cock and guide it firmly into Kate's willing pussey. I found the mark at once as with a squelch, his thick shaft passed between her cunney lips and he began to pump in and out as the juices eased his passage.

As I was still on all fours, my bum was high in the air, inviting itself to Johnny – which honestly had not occurred to me at that stage, although I knew immediately what my gallant spark had in mind when I felt his finger, wetted with champagne, cunningly insert itself between the cheeks of my bottom and into my luscious little crack. I raised my rounded globes so that the tiny wrinkled bum-hole was better exposed to his imminent attack.

I turned my head to see that dear Johnny had also stripped to the buff. He was also on his knees holding his proud cock which stood high, the rubicund red dome glistening from the sparkling wine with which he had annointed it. 'Ah, Jenny, such luscious, firm young cheeks, I must split them with my prick!' he declared and good as his word slewed his cock between my buttocks. One, two, three thrusts and he was inside me as he slid his strong arms around me to cup my breasts in his hands. Then he dropped his right hand down to insert his fingers in my cunt as he worked in and out of my arse-hole. The motions of my bottom, caused by the fall of Johnny's thighs against my backside, made me frig myself on his fingers thus enabling me to enjoy a double pleasure. But the nervous nippings and contractions of my bum-hole were too exciting and before I could experience a full spend, Johnny squirted a stream of hot spunk into my bottom. He cursed having spent too quickly though his cock was still thick as, POP, he withdrew it, like a cork leaving a bottle, from my bum-hole.

In the meantime, next to us, Harold and Kate were still engaged in their voluptuous fuck. Her legs were now wrapped around him as he continued to piston his hips up and down as Kate goaded him to further heights. 'Push on, push on, aaaah, aaaah, what a big, big, prick, aaah, give me more Harold, bang your big cock in and out of my juicy cunney!' Harold complied vigorously, burying his cock to the hilt as his balls flopped against her heaving buttocks. His movements became faster and faster until with a scream, he exploded into her, filling her cunney with spasm after spasm of hot love-juice as Kate too shuddered into a fine climax as the lovers jerked away in new paroxysms of delight, panting and sucking until they sank back, sated, upon the bed.

This had whet my own appetite for a good fuck so I kissed Johnny lightly on the lips and this was enough of a signal that I needed his immediate attention. Our mouths meshed together and putting his tongue in my mouth, he explored the top half between the teeth and gums that lifted my lips right up. His hands roamed over my breasts and he squeezed the hard little titties until I thought I would come straight away.

But he descended below and reached my sopping muff where his fingers seemed to spend an unconscionable time. My cunt lips were now soaking wet with anticipation. His huge prick was throbbing wildly as I cupped my hands around it, my creamy high-tipped breasts swinging over his face.

I circled my hands round that lovely cock which already had a blob of milky, sticky fluid at the end of the knob as I jammed down the foreskin and swooped low, lashing my tongue around the huge pole. Meanwhile, his lips had found my titties and I was concerned that he would again spend too soon. So I stopped sucking his cock and lay back on the bed, filching a pillow from behind Kate's head to stuff underneath my bottom so as I threw open my legs, Johnny was given a fair view of my waiting slit.

'Fuck me, Johnny!' I commanded and the sweet boy obeyed me at the instant. I felt his cock nudge against me, juiced up so that his cock slipped in easily as my own love juice dribbled down my thighs.

He started pumping into me with swinging thrusts as my arse arched up and down to receive his delicious rod and we fucked happily away, his cock plunging deeper and deeper until my legs left the bed to wrap themselves around his back as my hands clutched his shoulders as he suddenly became rigid and I could feel his build-up coming as his hairy balls slapped hard against my thighs. As his climax juddered to boiling point, I felt the throb of liquid fire rage inside me with every throb of that divine cock as his creamy froth spurted and spurted into me and my own orgasm came in a rush as my saturated clitty sent shudders of pleasure throughout my entire body.

Harold turned down the lights and under the dark anonymity of the sheets we played until the early hours. Kate and I sucked up the boys' cocks to new heights and I let Harold suck my tits whilst Johnny fucked my bottom and Jenny licked out my pussey. What a wild, uninhibited night we enjoyed at the Jim-Jam Club and my crack was so sore that I walked somewhat unsteadily from the carriage to Aunt Portia's front door.

I hope there will be a further opportunity to visit the Club, especially for the *récherché* Victor Pudendum entertainment. Harold, Johnny and Kate agreed with me that watching a sexual act enhanced one's own appetite for action. I understand that the next contest takes place in a fortnight or so and I shall ensure, if I possibly can, that I shall be in the audience, cheering on the players as they take the stage.

August 18th, 1871

I am feeling quite exhausted, diary dearest, even though it is only half past ten o'clock. I have made my excuses to Aunt Portia and Lord and Lady Bracknell who were dining quietly with us tonight and have retired early to my room.

Perhaps it is the exertions of previous days that have so tired me but I think it has been the boredom of a day and night without the comforting arms of Johnny Oaklands around me that have reduced me to such a listless state.

Be that as it may, I must record my grateful thanks at the continual refusal of Aunt Portia to insist on my taking a chaperone with me. I was invited to tea by Beatrice Billton this afternoon and she was stunned – and candidly admitted to feeling terribly envious of my freedom.

'You see, Papa,' she cried, 'Jenny's aunt trusts her to walk through a respectable area alone or drive out by herself in a carriage.

'Is it that you and other parents do not trust your daughters when out of your sight to behave in a rational and ladylike manner? Or is it that you believe that I and other young unmarried ladies do not possess enough presence of mind to find our way about the streets, to avoid being run over by omnibuses perhaps, or to be able to count out a shilling for a cabby? If so, this is to be deplored. But even worse is what I believe to be the real reason and that is the constantly repeated formula "People would talk so if . . ."'

'I hope Jenny has not been putting any rebellious thoughts in your pretty little head,' said Sir George Billton in a portentous tone of voice.

'I have said nothing on this subject before to Beatrice,' I

answered, somewhat stung by his implied rebuke, 'although I agree with every word she has spoken.'

'It is such a trifling concern, however,' piped up Lady Billton. 'After all, does it much matter whether a girl goes out alone or is accompanied by a chaperone?'

'It may be a trifling requirement,' I replied, 'but as the philosopher said, the world is made up of trifles and these are trifles that cause an incredible amount of discontent, grumbling and irritation.'

Beatrice nodded her head and said: 'We are bound, Mama, by so many senseless prejudices, meaningless restrictions and annoying trammels.'

'I don't know what you want and I wonder whether you do,' rejoined Sir George. 'You have a good home, every comfort and the society of our friends. You have all the luxuries of modern life. What more can you possible desire?'

'Dear Papa, I am afraid that you just do not understand. Do you not see that I would gladly engage in any honourable labour, however menial, to enable myself to be independent and to own myself. Now I walk in your paths but I need the freedom to walk in those I freely choose to take. How would you like to have no independence but be obliged always to live someone else's life and always have to beg for your sustenance. For the woman, this sad state carries through even when she is married when she is at the beck and call of her husband.'

'Stuff and nonsense!' declared Sir George. 'The normal relationship inside marriage between husband and wife must be the normal one of control and decision on the husband's side and deference and submission on that of the wife's.'

'Do you really believe that, Lady Billton?' I asked incredulously.

'Oh, yes, my dear. As the old saying has it, "Where two ride on a horse, one must needs ride behind."'

Beatrice groaned: 'You should hear our arguments upon

women obtaining the franchise. She genuinely thinks that such a step would be a retrograde development!'

'I do not oppose social progress simply because I always plump for the status quo,' said Lady Billton with a hint of annoyance creeping into her tone. 'Woman, as she has been bequeathed to us in the past, is recognized as too precious an inheritance to be tampered with in light fashion. The dread lest any change in the conditions which have given us this inheritance should desecrate this inheritance is both wise and worthy.'

'Indeed it is so, my love,' agreed Sir George. 'And we can hope for nothing better than that the strong voice of sensible opinion will always be raised against any innovations of culture that may tend to spoil the sweet efflorescence of evolution.'

There was little point in continuing the argument so I said that I must agree to disagree and asked permission of this pompous pair to take a stroll round the large half-acre garden with Beatrice.

'Indeed you may,' said Sir George, and adding, as he no doubt wished to appear magnanimous in a victory that he never achieved, 'and you don't need a chaperone whilst together on our own property.'

The weather was still warm although the sun now hid beneath a curtain of cloud so we did not need the benefit of parasols to protect our faces from its harmful rays.

'I so envy you, dear Jenny,' said Beatrice. 'My parents are so fuddy-duddy in their thinking that I do believe I shall go quite mad if I have to exist in this state for much longer.'

'Are they so strict?' I asked.

'They just cannot understand how I suffer from possessing no money in my own right and being obliged to ask, admittedly from a not always unwilling parent, for any and every thing. I have been quiet and uncomplaining up till now but in future I am determined to enjoy myself how I wish just as my brother does. You know my brother Reginald? He is one year younger than I yet he enjoys everything I seem destined never to enjoy. I can never sit down to read or write without being disturbed. But Reggie, who is reading at home during his vacation, is never to be interrupted. I cannot be trusted with money but Reggie possesses an allowance. Where is the justice in all this?'

Her reasoning could not be faulted and I attempted to comfort her with some encouraging words of future happiness. But what could I say? Then I had a brainwave.

'Tell me, Beatrice,' I said carefully, 'was what you said about never being able to meet members of the opposite sex true or, if not a falsehood, perhaps a slight exaggeration?'

The sweet girl blushed and looked around to ensure that we were truly alone before she answered: 'The remark was basically true, Jenny, but there have been occasions when I have managed to slip out of the overfirm fist of parental might.'

'Oh, ho,' I giggled. 'Who then is the lucky young man who has been so favoured?'

'His name is Archie Rice, a college friend of Reginald, my brother.'

'Archie Rice, Archie Rice,' I blurted out. 'Wait a moment, I do believe I know the young man. Is he one of the Wiltshire Rices?'

'That's right, Jenny, how coincidental that you two have met.'

Well, it was a coincidence but as she spoke, I was wishing that I had not imparted this information for reasons that will become obvious as I continue the record of the conversation.

'Yes,' I said slowly, 'I made his acquaintance back home at Major Ronne's Charity Ball in Aid of the Local Hospitals. He is certainly a very good-looking boy.' I forsook to mention that this good-looking young ruffian had squeezed my bum whilst we were dancing the military two step and gave my left breast an equally affectionate touch during the valeta.

'He is a nice boy,' sighed Beatrice. 'I enjoy Archie's

company immensely but I am so ignorant about matters of the world that I fear he will soon stop paying attention to me.

'You see, he comes round at least twice a week ostensibly to discuss work with Reggie. But my brother is a sport and he always leaves Archie and me together in the billiard-room which is the most suitable place to meet as Papa cannot play until his bout of sciatica dies down so we can talk and, er, yes talk in private.'

'Beatrice,' I said with a mock sternness, 'come, do not prevaricate with me! We are old friends and any secret you deposit with me is as safe as if it were in the Bank of England!'

She looked around again and seeing that we were alone, she said softly: 'Well, we have kissed and cuddled, Jenny, and I am telling you this, Jenny, because I would value some advice. Tell me, have you ever let a man caress your bosom?'

I gave a gay little laugh. 'Of course I have, many times. I love having my bosoms caressed and squeezed whilst I am engaged in an amorous embrace. There is nothing wrong about that! Don't feel guilty about it!'

'I don't!' said Beatrice. 'But Archie is not satisfied with feeling my bubbies through my dress. He wants to undo the buttons on my blouse and caress my bare breasts. And, oh, Jenny, I would love to feel his hand on my naked skin but I have never plucked up the courage to let him do it. You see, I am a virgin and wish to remain so until I feel I am ready to enjoy the delights of sexual intercourse, which I understand are bounteous. I am frightened that if I let Johnny feel my titties, he will take further liberties and become so inflamed that I shall not be able to resist his desires and be ruined forever!'

I did not want to tell Beatrice, who was so unschooled in *l'arte de faire l'amour*, of my own far more hectic experiences than having one's bosom touched. So I said truthfully that she should not feel pressured into taking part in any action with which she did not feel happy. 'However,' I said, 'I have progressed further down this avenue than you and am more than happy to instruct you.'

'Oh, Jenny, would you please? I am such a noodle and I really would like to learn.'

'Very well, then. Your first lesson must be to enjoy yourself. You can only do this if you have absolute trust in your man. Before you begin to embrace you must warn him that you do not wish to take matters to their ultimate conclusion and he must obey your command to desist if he goes too far. To begin with, make sure you have an avenue of escape if Archie proves to be a cad. Do lock the door but ensure there are people in the house who would hear your upraised voice if need be.

'On the other hand, I do not think that cock-teasing is a proper sport for a lady. You should always ensure that your man obtains the release of spunking – I hope my forthright words do not offend, but in the country, we call a spade a spade.'

'No, no, not at all. Reggie keeps copies of smutty magazines and I have come across them by accident. And I must say they were exciting to read!' said Beatrice, who paused for a moment and then continued: 'Jenny, Archie is with Reggie at this very moment. Look, there they are, waving to us from Reggie's rooms. They want us to come upstairs. Shall we do so? We can sneak in through the back door and my parents will not know!'

It was indeed all too easy to fulfil this assignation. I knew Reggie only slightly and when Beatrice and Archie went off to the billiard-room, I let Reggie know that I was going out with Johnny Oaklands and that I was unavailable for larks. He was so disappointed that he said: 'Then I am going back into my rooms to study. You may do as you like.' So I walked softly across the landing to the billiard room and rather crossly I saw that Beatrice had ignored my very first important piece of advice to lock the door, which was slightly ajar. I could not resist peeping in and sure enough, there were the two young love birds, sitting on the smooth cushion of the billiard table and kissing in a most passionate manner. I am a firm believer that nature herself guides the way for inexperienced young lovers, and for sure, Archie was by no means clumsy in the way he was undoing Beatrice's blouse.

Their ardour was so intent that they did not hear me enter and softly close the door behind me and turn the key in the lock.

Archie had now shrugged off Beatrice's blouse and was opening her chemise to reveal a lovely pair of soft rounded globes, each tipped with large aureoles and pointed nipples which seemed to harden before Archie covered them with his hands. Beatrice let herself be pushed down upon the table and Archie worked his way down her gorgeous creamy body. She gasped with astonished fright as he found the opening of her skirt and quickly unleashed it so she was clad only in white frilly drawers and her stockings. Whether by accident or design I do not know but her long slim legs were already slightly parted as his hand reached down between them and began to rub her mons Veneris through the thin material of her drawers.

'Oh, Archie, Archie, you mustn't, you really mustn't do that. Remember what I told you, I don't want to lose my virginity.'

'I promise you that I shall respect your wishes,' hissed the handsome youth, untying the lace of her knickers and trying to pull them off until Beatrice rebuked him and broke off the embrace.

'Archie, you are a rude boy,' responded Beatrice. 'But I mean what I say. Jenny Everleigh told me I was right not to let you have your way with me though she said I had to give you relief. The trouble is, I don't know how to.'

'Is that what Jenny said? I suppose you girls always stick together though she is quite right about giving me relief. Shall I show you how to do it?'

Beatrice nodded so with a smile Archie dropped his trousers and unknown to him, two girls were avidly concentrating on the bulging front of his undershorts! When he slid them off, I gave an involuntary little cry. What a magnificent cock stood out from between his thighs. It was veined and hard as a rock, jutting up proudly with a giant, bulbous head. He rubbed his hand up and down the shaft and each time he pulled his foreskin to and fro, it made a juicy noise from the spunk that had already leaked out in his excitement.

Archie had not heard my little gasp but Beatrice had and she looked wildly around as she whispered: 'Archie, there's someone here!'

I stepped forward so as not to alarm them further and said: 'It is only me, Jenny, don't be afraid. I didn't mean to interrupt you but you forgot the first rule – always lock the door! Don't be embarrassed, I'll leave as quietly as I came in.'

'No, don't leave us, Jenny,' said Beatrice. 'I am still not sure how to give Archie the relief you told me he needs so perhaps you can show me what to do if necessary.'

'What a splendid idea!' said Archie, his eyes gleaming. 'You cannot refuse your friend this request as after all you advised her as to her mode of conduct.'

'Very well, then,' I said, 'I'll stay but just forget about me and carry on as if I were not here.'

They agreed to this and pretty soon were locked in a fine old embrace. Knowing that help was at hand if need be, Beatrice let Archie pull down her knickers and her moist, mossy grotto came into my view, with the little pink labia already fluttering out in anticipation of the joys to come. Archie pushed her legs apart as he separated her cunney lips with a questing forefinger, letting it slide up and down the full length of her pretty slit.

'Oooooh, Oooooh! Oh, Archie, it's wonderful!' gasped Beatrice as he worked slowly and surely in her pouting cunney-lips.

'I'm so pleased you like it,' panted Archie, whose proud prick was now rigidly erect. 'I just wish that someone would do something like that for me!'

How could I resist the invitation! In any case, it would be most instructive for Beatrice to see how a cock should be sucked.

'Beatrice, let me show you how to give Archie his relief,' I said, moving next to Archie and wetting my lips with my tongue. His eyes glistened in anticipation when I grasped his broad cock by the shaft. I pulled the foreskin back to reveal an almost purple knob. I was on my knees in next to no time, huddled up as near as was comfortable for me to grasp his bulky tool at the base. I kissed the dewy top and licked my tongue around the rim.

'Jenny, that was just too wonderful,' said Archie, now popping his fingers in and out of Beatrice's juicy cunt. 'I want you to suck all the sperm out of my balls.'

So I thoroughly wet the top of his cock and opening my mouth, I slipped the knob end in. The taste was deliciously salty with that unique masculine tang. I closed my lips around it as tight as I could and worked on the knob with my tongue, easing my lips forward to take in gradually a little more of the shaft. I still circled the base of his prick with my hand and then began to work the loose skin up and down and at the same time began to bob my head up and down. I sucked and sucked on that delicious cock until it almost touched the back of my throat.

Archie was now really excited and his hips lifted off the table into the air as my licking and sucking increased in tempo. I cupped his balls, feeling them harden and sure enough his rigid shaft jerked and spurted out jets of creamy spunk. The jet hit the back of my throat and as any girl who has sucked cocks will tell you, diary, it is hard to swallow with your mouth full of gushing sperm. But practice makes perfect and I swallowed the wonderful flood of salty spend until the jets eased off into a dribble.

Beatrice was now coming in a series of quivers and Archie's fingers were coated with cunney juice.

'That's how you give your man relief if you don't want to fuck!' I said to Beatrice.

'I'm more than willing to try,' she rejoined, 'but look at poor Archie's prick. It is all shriven up and is quite flaccid.'

'Well, what do you expect?' snapped Archie. 'No one can keep a hard-on after being sucked off so expertly as that. But there is a way in which you can swiftly make my prick swell up again.

'Jenny, lick out Beatrice's pussey! I want to see you suck up her cunney juices. She'll love it, won't you, Beatrice?'

Beatrice nodded her assent and my blood was up so I pulled the nude girl onto my lap and we pressed our lips together, wiggling our tongues in our mouths until I moved mine down to her firm young breasts, twirling my tongue round each engorged nipple in turn. Her skin was so soft that I thoroughly enjoyed letting my tongue travel the length of her velvety body, lingering only briefly at her belly button before sliding down to the insides of her thighs. I moved in to nuzzle my lips between her swollen cunney lips that were already oozing juice and I sucked upon the hardening little clitty, flicking my tongue in and out of her lovely little hairy quim, sucking and slurping the juices from her heated cunt, filling the air with the scent of sex.

The sweet girl was now writhing in ecstacy as I pushed my mouth hard up against her, moving my entire head back and forth. She was now drenching my mouth with torrents of juice and I knew that I was playing the right notes upon her delicate instrument. She came in a series of little quivers and I raised my head slightly to see that Archie was becoming very excited.

He began to play with himself, capping and uncapping the knob of his swelling cock, and between the reaction I was getting from Beatrice and the sight of this burgeoning, bulky prick, I too was becoming aroused and I felt my own pussey dampening and the juice dribbling through into my knickers.

Archie rubbed away furiously at his swollen cock and I was concerned that he would spend before poor Beatrice could suck his prick! So I took my mouth out of her honeypot and murmured: 'Now then, Beatrice, kiss his cock!' The brave girl smiled at me and wetting her lips as she had seen me do a few minutes before, she swooped down onto his gloriously hard truncheon. She swallowed at least three inches of thick prick – she obviously needed to further, the girl was a natural cocksucker. Archie groaned and his staff twitched convulsively with joy as the slurping of Beatrice's tongue proclaimed that he had enjoyed a second copious spend. But as I have just written, it is extremely difficult for a novice to swallow the juice whilst it is still jetting into the mouth, and some frothy elixir bubbled out of her mouth. I knelt down in front of them and gripped Archie's cock, which was still full if not at the peak of its stiffness, lifted it up and licked his balls clean with my saliva. I tried to suck his prick up to a third cockstand but alas, the spirit was willing but the flesh was weak and we had to finish our little *ménage à trois* on this slightly unsatisfactory note.

I had spent in my knickers which were now very wet and most uncomfortable but when I mentioned this to Beatrice she insisted on lending me a pair of her own. Archie went downstairs by himself to allay any parental suspicion whilst Beatrice and I crossed the landing to her bedroom.

I raised my dress to take down my drawers and Beatrice said: 'Let me put these new ones on for you, Jenny. But first, here is a towel, let me dry your wet little cranny.' She sank to her knees in front of me and raised my dress, peering up to see what lay above.

'My, what smooth skin you have, Jenny, and what a silky growth of blonde hair curls around your grotto. And such lovely pink moist pussey lips,' she said, running her busy hands up to my mound, skimming my cunt with her knuckles. 'Your cunt has an aching need to be kissed, to be explored, to be entered, to be filled . . .' she murmured, and clutching my buttocks and raising her body up, she licked her way up to my cunney, sucking and chewing whilst diddling my cranny with her left hand and wrapping her right arm across my bum. She then released my bum to gently caress my cunt as her kisses reached my motte and her tongue parted my cunt lips, licking fervently at my juices. Very quickly, I sensed I was going to spend and I climaxed beautifully as she kissed and sucked my sopping pussey.

Not till she had drained every drop of juice from me did my saucy friend condescend to dry my wet cunney with her towel. I slipped on the new knickers kindly loaned to me and we made our way downstairs. Fortunately Sir George and Lady Billton had decided to take a stroll. Archie and Reginald had opened a bottle of whiskey and had consumed a goodly amount when we arrived in the drawing room.

I dislike men who cannot hold their liquor and it was plain to see that the two men were determined to finish the bottle, which would leave them quite intoxicated. So I bade them farewell, saying (falsely) that I had to go home to change as that evening I was attending a concert by Signorina Rosa Marchiano, the great star of the Italian Opera.

'I know a good song,' leered Reginald, 'but I don't think Signorina Marchiano will be singing it! You know it, Archie, old boy, all about Poor Old Sally. Let us sing the chorus for the girls – one, two, three . . .' and they began caterwauling a current music hall song which went something like this:

She may have known better days when she was in her prime,
She may have known better days once upon a time.
But then one day she fell from grace and so stands alone to hunt,
She sells some flowers, any old thing, but most of all her cunt!

September 22nd, 1871

The Season is well under way; and I have been to so many parties! Night after night there have been receptions, galas, parties of all description. Truly, life has been all balls!

Today, dear diary, I must recount the very funny happenings last night at Colonel Norbert and Lady Netherspoon's ball. Over the past weeks, there was a considerable part of youthful London Society at least that had the ball of the gallant Colonel and his wife (she is Aunt Portia's sister-in-law, incidentally) on their lips. Not confined to one sex was the interest taken in this grand function. The tattle of tea-tables was supplemented by the gossip of clubs, and what to wear and who was to wear it greatly exercised the parishes of St James and St George.

As next to making ourselves ridiculous the greatest pleasure is to see our friends doing the same, the intimation that fancy, court dress or uniform was *de riguer* gave the highest satisfaction. The well-known munificence of the host, well known for his charitable works and (as I was to find out) something a little less known to all but his closest, most intimate friends, prepared the mind of society for something out of the common.

Diary, there are balls and balls and I have seen many banks of flowers, the diamond crusted tiaras, the small supper tables, the music of Colin and Allan and all the rest of it. But I saw something in the gilded rooms of the Metropole that was to eclipse all this. The company was distinguished, the decorations handsome but not overdone. The ballroom decorations, with the prominent 'N' and its double significance for Norbert and Netherspoon were in excellent taste.

The costumes were admirable. Johnny had come dressed as a North American Indian and I was dressed as a squaw, my skirt far higher than would normally be considered proper and the swell of my bosom was clearly delineated through the tight fitting cotton of my cotton top. Both of us sported magnificent head-dresses with coloured feathers (we bought the costumes on loan from Aspiso the theatrical costumiers as did many other guests). We were not the only Red Indians and there were enough of us to form a veritable tribe of savages!

Colonel Norbert led young Lady Pettitt in the procession to the supper-room, followed by a multitude from the courts of the great Harry, the second Charles, the fourteenth and fifteenth Louis with attendant Pompadours, Borgias, Knights of Jerusalem – and many, many others.

The supper and wine were absolutely spiffing and, as I can never fib in these pages, I must set down the fact that several guests, including Johnny and myself, were somewhat worse the wear after what must have been the ninth bottle of champagne was opened at our table.

After the meal, while the tables were being cleared away, I went to the ladies room to relieve my bursting bladder. Johnny also afforded himself the same luxury and we arranged to meet afterwards in the Godfrey Suite.

I made my way through the throng of fancy-dressed guests and had my bum pinched three times, once I am sure by HRH The Prince of Wales who had come to the ball as Henry VIII.

The Godfrey Suite was situated on the first floor and though not out of bounds to the guests, few of them knew of the existence of the semi-private small lounge. The room was almost in darkness with only a small table light glowing softly when I opened the heavy door. I heard the buzz of conversation and through the smokey haze, for at least two gentlemen there were puffing away on cigars, saw a Red Indian bonnet with the fine collection of feathers above the back of a chair.

For some strange reason I stayed standing by the door and did not walk across the room immediately. To my horror, I saw a pretty girl dressed as Nell Gwynne stand up in front of the chair where the Red Indian was sitting, undo the front of her blouson and let free a pair of well-formed, uptilted breasts which were topped by small, dark nipples. To a muted chorus of approval, she stepped out of her skirt and pulled off her white drawers leaving herself stark naked as she gracefully began to move her hands lasciviously down her slim body. I recognized her pretty face as none other than Victoria Hawley-Pratte whose family were good friends of Johnny's and who had made eyes at Johnny at Cecily Worthing's nineteenth birthday party just two weeks before!

Admittedly, she was a most attractive girl with flowing dark locks, a most seductive full mouth though her figure was rather coltish with small but pert breasts, a smooth, flat belly at the base of which grew a luxuriant thatch of curly dark hair that set off her long legs. Now I could see the Red Indian kick off his boots and struggling to divest himself of his leggings. As the chair was at a slight angle to my view, I could not see his face or torso as he slumped down in his seat. But I could see Victoria kneeling down in front of him and taking an erect cock in her hands and massaging it up and down on her flat palms. As soon as she had judged the penis to be at its fullest height she moved her head forward to take the prick into her mouth. The touch of her lips and tongue were too much for the Red Indian who leaned back and groaned as she sucked lustily away with uninhibited slurps. She sucked hard, taking at least half the shaft into her mouth whilst her hands played with his balls. She sucked with a firm motion then slid her wet lips up and down the rock-hard cockshaft, gulping noisily as the tool slid along the roof of her mouth to the back of her throat.

Her naked bottom cheeks wriggled provocatively as she left off sucking her sweetmeat for a moment as she called out, 'Well, come on somebody, I want a nice thick cock shooting spunk up my bum!'

And who should be first to undo his trousers and stand behind her with an erect cock standing stiffly out between his shirt-tails but out host, the genial Colonel Norbert! His pego was not the thickest I have seen but it made up for thickness by its length for it must have been at least nine inches long. He took hold of his pulsating shaft and eased the gleaming shaft between those rounded arse cheeks that were jutting out, simply asking to be split. He moistened the uncapped dome with spittle and his long shaft quickly enveloped itself between the rolling cheeks of that delicious bum.

As befitted an officer and a gentleman, the Colonel pushed slowly at first, but Victoria brought her hand round to open her legs wider without falling or losing grip of either the prick in her mouth or the prick in her bum. 'Ah, that's well in, my game little filly!' cried the Colonel, bending over Victoria to fondle the erect little nipples on her swinging breasts. There was no doubt of Vicky's total enjoyment as the Colonel pounded in and out of her adorable bum whilst she sucked greedily on the cock in her mouth which looked ready to jet out its load of cream. And stream it did, as she swallowed the copious draught of spunk whilst, with a cry of delight, the good Colonel flooded her arsehole with spout after spout of juicy sperm, filling her hole as with a succulent POP, he withdrew his glistening shaft and wiped away the last drops of white cum from the tip.

As far as I was concerned, if Colonel Norbert wanted to take the chance of his wife coming in whilst he was in *flagrante delicto*, this was his affair. But I was most annoyed with Johnny for letting Vicky suck him off. I would have been pleased to suck his cock although not, I may say, in full view of at least seven or eight strangers.

What is sauce for the goose is sauce for the gander, I decided, and without a second thought, quickly disrobed until I too was quite naked. A man dressed as Charles II was looking lasciviously at me. He must have been Vicky's partner as she had come as Nell Gwynne! He, lucky fellow, would receive an unexpected party treat tonight!

Never mind that I had never seen this man – who looked the very image of the Merry Monarch in his costume – I was determined to let myself be fucked by a total stranger in front of Johnny to let him see that two could play at his game.

Yes, of course it was an impetuous, childish gesture but I was so angry that I tore open my blouse and lifted out my large breasts, tweaking up my titties with my own fingers. I boldly sat down on the side arm of the chair where this good looking Charles II sat and thrust my breasts up to an inch of his nose!

'Here, Your Majesty,' I said, 'try my melons. I'm sure you will find them far sweeter than Nell Gwynne's oranges!'

I took hold of my left tittie and proferred it to his mouth. At first his mouth fell open in astonishment but when it was obvious that the offer was genuine, he began to nibble and suck my tittie which began to make my pussey tingle in anticipation. I sat down on his lap and the sight and feel of my nude body had the required effect and I felt his cock stiffening beneath me. I moved over slightly to allow him to suck my other tittie and I put my hand on his rod and gave the swelling shaft a friendly rub through the thin satin material of his trousers.

'Let's not let a piece of satin come between friends,' I said, and unbuttoned his trousers and felt inside for his hard cock which sprang out like a released coil. My pussey was now wet and his hand worked his way down to my mound, moving between the lips of my slit to my fast hardening clitty. I clasped his hand between my legs as I lowered my head to kiss the uncapped dome of his nice-looking prick. But after a quick lick I lifted my head and said, 'Your Majesty, I think we could enjoy this better if you divested yourself of your clothes.'

'I believe you are right, squaw,' he grinned. 'Just let me get up for a moment and I will oblige.'

He quickly shed his clothes and I admired his good looks, his firm, manly chest and fine torso and of course a fine hard cock which stood up to attention almost flat up against his belly. We smiled and then we embraced, our tongues meshing together before slipping into each other's mouths. He let his hands drop onto my bum cheeks and he gripped them as he firmly pressed my pussey against his rockhard cock which he rubbed hard against me.

I was enjoying this though I felt guilty about performing in public. But now I was reckless with desire as I took his hand and rubbed it against my crack. I was now ready so I carefully lay down on the floor and opened my legs wide, giving him and the other men who had now crowded round a good view. I spread open the lips of my aching cunney, revealing the glistening insides of my pink love channel. He knelt between my legs and aimed his gorgeous cock at me. First he rubbed the tip of my clitty, jerking me up and taking me almost to the brink of spending.

'You would like me to fuck you?' he asked.

'Yes, yes, yes, put your cock right up my cunt!' I panted. He rolled me over onto my front and realising what he wanted I lay my head on one side on the carpet and pushed out my bum. I felt his hand on my buttocks, parting them to let his shaft sink into my eager cunney. He eased it in and out, his arms wrapped round me and his hands busy playing around my aroused titties. I pushed back onto his rigid shaft wanting more and more and the quicker he thrust the wilder became my responses. 'Faster,' I yelled, 'faster!' He duly obliged, quickening his pace, and his prick pulsed and twitched until with a final tremble he shot a torrent of hot froth inside me. Soon he was panting hard as my cunney milked him of the last drops of his spendings.

'You haven't spent yet, have you?' he queried.

'I am afraid not, sire,' I replied, 'but that does not matter.'

'Yes, it jolly well does,' he replied sternly, 'it is always best if both partners enjoy the fuck equally.' So he sank down beside me and inserted his head between my legs and, quickly inserting his tongue between my cunney lips, immediately found my still swollen clitty. He began to frig me fast with two fingers with his face pressed up against my slit as I began to roll from side to side as again he began to lick, harder and harder, making me scream with delight as I reached the ultimate peak and love juices exploded out of me, mingling with the spunk that was dribbling down my legs.

There was a ripple of applause from the onlookers. 'Perhaps we should have charged for admission,' he said to me as we began to put back our clothes. 'But tell me, who are you and why did you suddenly choose to fuck me without so much as a by-your-leave?'

'Ny name is Jenny Everleigh. What's yours?'

'I'm Lord Gerfoyle,' said the handsome young man. 'Now how about answering the second part of my question.'

'Oh, why I wanted to be fucked by you? Well, my lord, your partner was sucking off my partner as I came in and –'

'Hold hard, who's your partner?'

'Johnny Oaklands, he's dressed as a Red Indian. He was sitting down in that chair –'

'He was NOT,' snapped Johnny's voice just behind me. 'I was waylaid coming up here by Lady Beaver and when I arrived you were sitting on Lord Gerfoyle's lap, sucking his cock!'

I flushed red with embarrassment. 'Oh, Johnny, I am most dreadfully sorry.'

'I'm not!' interrupted Lord Gerfoyle cheerfully. 'I had a most wonderful fuck and the other gentleman almost enjoyed the performance as much as we enjoyed taking part.'

'That's not the point,' I said slowly. 'But Johnny, if you weren't here before, who is the Red Indian who Vicky sucked off?'

'James Burman, at your service,' called out a voice, 'and if you would like to fuck me, Miss Everleigh, please do not hesitate. My address is Flat 69, East Court, Green Street.'

I followed the direction of the voice and sure enough there stood a young man of Johnny's build, resplendent in exactly the same outfit as Johnny!

'From Mr Edwards at Aspiso's?' said Johnny.

'Absolutely, old boy, I picked it up this morning.'

What a sweet boy Johnny Oaklands is, diary, for seeing that a genuine mistake had been made, he made our apologies and we left the room to go to the main ballroom. As we waltzed around the floor, I asked Johnny how Lord Gerfoyle could be happy to let his partner for the evening, young Vicky, suck off Mr Burman in front of his face.

'Oh, he's an odd bod,' said Johnny. 'Whilst he was a Sandhurst cadet he proposed to a Miss Bertha Finney, the daughter of an artisan of that name who was playing in that new play at the Savoy Theatre.

'He was accepted and Lord and Lady Putney, his parents, with reluctance sanctioned the engagement which, however, Lord Gerfoyle subsequently broke off, under pressure it seems from his parents though this excuse cut no ice when Miss Finney went to the High Court. She was awarded ten thousand pounds damages!'

September 25th, 1871

Such an exciting night, dear diary! Aunt Portia had to wake me herself at eleven o'clock this morning for I did not arrive home until almost five and I was so over-tired that it was fast approaching dawn when I finally entered the soothing arms of Morpheus.

What an evening! I am concerned as to whether I should record the exact happenings at the Jim-Jam Club as surely posterity will never know (except from your pages) about the famed Victor Pudendum contest. Should I tell or should I remain silent? After all, there are reputations at stake . . . I shall pause for thought and let the muse decide.

I have thought long and hard about this, diary, and I have concluded that it would be best to reveal all – tell the truth and shame the devil, as the old saying has it. Johnny Oaklands will not be discomforted, nor indeed will Harold Le Meshigunah and Nathan Wabolowski, although Simeon Scott may not be too pleased at my decision to recount this extraordinary tale.

Enough chatter, dear diary, let us move from the *hors d'oeuvres* to the main course.

In case you had forgotten, diary, the Victor Pudendum is a fucking contest held monthly at the Jim-Jam Club in aid of charity – all profits from the event are distributed to the Society for the Propagation of Useful Knowledge to the Poor People of London. Entrants (who are restricted to members of the Jim-Jam or their nominated guests) are required to fuck their partners in front of a selected audience. An entrance fee of one hundred guineas per pair was payable plus another twenty-five guineas payable to the lady of pleasure (recruited from the highest class of girls plying their trade from either Mrs Hannington's Night-House in the Haymarket or the 'millinery' owned by Mrs Wickley-Featherstonehaugh in Grafton Street, Mayfair.) Entrants are judged upon their style, grace and other such attributes by a distinguished panel of judges and a gold cup is presented to the winner and a purse of one hundred sovereigns is presented to the girl. The entrance fee (which includes two bottles of champagne and light refreshments) is fifty pounds a head and there is always a huge demand for tickets.

Fortunately, Harold Le Meshigunah had bribed Dodds, the chief attendant at the Jim-Jam, to secure us one of the tables at the front of the square where all the action was to take place. I should perhaps explain that the Victor Pudendum takes place in the Club's large dining room. The tables were arranged so that the centre of the room was cleared except for a large mattress which was placed on a special bed built especially for the affair (the brainchild, incidentally, of Major Puxley whilst serving out in Poona some thirty-five years before). This bed had a special small headboard so that pillows might be fluffed up upon it but an excellent view might still be afforded to spectators behind it.

Indeed, that place – behind the headboard – was where the three judges sat, each with a small side-table, to mark the performers' efforts. The judges last night were Harknett Hughes, the painter and connoisseur: Oscar Wilde, the man of letters; and Sir Miller Moss, the well-known sportsman whose chestnut mare Clare had the day before won a six hundred pound race at Sandown Park.

Some ten tables were placed around the sides and foot of the bed (ours was one of the best, so that we were level with the centre of the bed) and behind the tables there was standing room for another thirty or so gentlemen. Until 1868, the audience was solely comprised of the masculine sex but since HRH decided to bring Lady Clare B------ so as to whet her appetite for a royal frolic *a deux*, a select number of women have been allowed to watch the proceedings.

Whilst waiting for Sir Jaspar Muttlebury to begin the business of the evening, I looked up to the ceiling and for the first time noticed the ceiling upon which had been painted a most colourful, erotic fantasy. The centrepiece depiction was of an immense cunt, from between the lips of which extended a large carved prick, with balls attached from which hung a magnificent chandelier. And in keeping with the spirit of the evening, the silver goblets from which we sipped our beautifully cold champagne were shaped like pricks whilst the bowls in which the fruit was served were in the shape of cunneys, supported on exquisitely formed legs. At our table were Johnny and myself; Harold and a pretty new girl-friend, one Naomi from Tottenham Court Road whom he had picked up in Piccadilly whilst browsing through the stock at a bookshop; and Nathan Wabolowski, who was squiring another old friend of Harold's, Esme, a plump yet attractive French wench who had been living until recently with Simeon Scott, a past winner several times over of tonight's trophy.

At ten o'clock precisely, Sir Jaspar took up his position at the foot of the bed and called for silence.

'My Lord, ladies and gentlemen,' he cried out in stentorian tones, 'I bid you welcome to the Jim-Jam Club for the September Victor Pudendum Contest.

'We have four couples to contest for the September Gold Cup. In order of appearance, they are Sir Angus Walls and Nancy; Mr Wilson Brown and Caroline; The Honourable Cecil Knightley and Florence; and for the first time in the history of the Victor Pudendum, nominated by Sir Heddon Court, an artisan entrant, Joseph Hill, a native of Jamaica now in Sir Heddon's service, who will copulate with that noble lady known to many members, and who has indeed known many members (laughter and applause), the one and only Nelly from Windmill Street!'

A buzz of eager anticipatory gossip sprang through the

room. Who was this Negro servant of Sir Heddon? Was common tale of Negro prowess correct or mere rumour? I had heard that black men were often blessed wth large pricks and balls but never before had I been given the opportunity of testing this belief in an empiric manner. I am sure that many other guests were also mulling this over in their minds.

Sir Jaspar shouted: 'Dodds is standing by the door and will accept your wagers as to the winner and the runner-up. As the book now stands, Sir Angus is currently favourite at seven to four against; Mr Wilson Brown is seven to two against; the Honourable Cecil Knightley is five to one and Joseph Hill stands at eight to one. Place your bets, ladies and gentlemen. This is the final call for wagers on the Victor Pudendum – the contest will begin in precisely seven minutes.'

'Harold, are you going to wager?' enquired Johnny.

'I thought I might have a tenner on Sir Angus,' mused Monsieur Le Meshigunah. 'He has just returned to London from America where he spent two weeks in the Wild West and I heard him tell old Simeon Scott that he had not had a fuck since he left New York for the West. Even coming home, there was nothing for his prick except the five fingered widow, as you British put it.'

'Mind, old Angus is a Highland man and for all you know he may have shagged the sheep out in Texas,' laughed Johnny.

'Please, please, Johnny,' said Harold, taking his jest quite seriously, 'I partook of leg of lamb for luncheon and the thought of . . .'

His voice trailed off and Nathan Wabolowski grunted: 'That man there, isn't he Wilson Brown, who will follow your man? I understand that he is quite an athlete and has been in training for three weeks for the Victor Pudendum. He has been taking frequent exercise, eating and drinking sparingly and restricting his fucking to only three times a week.

'I shall put ten pounds on Mr Brown,' added Nathan.

'How about you, Jenny?' asked Harold. 'Perhaps you have the gift of feminine intuition that will enable you to pick the winner?'

I fumbled with my small handbag, but extracted my purse and took out three sovereigns. 'Johnny, put three pounds on the black man, Joseph Hill.'

'That's somewhat of a gamble, Jenny. We know nothing about him and besides he isn't a true-blue Englishman!' said Johnny.

'Do not be guilty of the sin of prejudice,' I responded. 'I am sure that Harold will agree that Englishmen have no divine prerogative to excellence in every human condition.'

Johnny smiled and held out his hand into which I dropped my three coins. He took ten pound notes from Harold and Nathan and strode across the room to place the bets with Dodds.

Soon after he returned the lights were dimmed and to a burst of applause the first couple, Angus and Nancy, took to the floor, bowing to the four corners of the room. They wore scarlet silk dressing gowns and made a handsome couple. Sir Angus was a tall gentleman of some thirty five years, well-built to the edge of corpulency (no doubt his predeliction for port was a major cause of this state) and Nancy too was of a somewhat Rubensesque stature.

They disrobed to a further small smattering of applause. Nancy was a not unattractive girl of twenty five or so years, plumpish as I have said with extremely large breasts topped by equally large aureoles and nipples. Her mound was covered with a profusion of rich brown hair and the swelling lips pouted most deliciously, the glowing red chink between looking most luxurious and inviting.

After a cheerful preliminary embrace, Nancy laid down on the bed, the pillows being propped up so that she could sit fairly straight with her legs wide open, presenting Angus with a fair mark. He took a deep breath, blew out his cheeks as he expelled the air from his lungs and took his strong-looking cock, which was of fair proportions, in his hand, and drawing back the foreskin, made the purple knob swell and bound in his hand.

His cock was heavy but not fully erect so Nancy heaved herself up and kneeling forward, pushing out the chubby cheeks of her bum and opening her legs to give the three judges an excellent view of both her arsehole and her cunt, grasped Angus's cock in her hands and slowly began to lick the red knob. The audience thrilled to see Angus's cock swell up to its full, majestic height and Nancy paused to give the shaft a good rub before taking the full length in her mouth until it must have been touching the back of her throat.

Slowly at first but then gradually working up to a neat rhythm, she began to suck noisily upon the fat cock, moving her head to and fro so that one moment the shaft was almost out of her mouth and the next was totally engulfed between her pouting lips, taking it all in almost up to his pubic hairs. Meanwhile, she gently squeezed his balls but as she felt Angus was too soon reaching the pinnacle of pleasure, she took his throbbing cock out of her mouth and no doubt with pre-arranged orchestration having been planned, kept tight hold of his prick until the handsome baronet was on the bed with her but flat on his back with his rampant pole sticking up proudly under her expert handling.

Nancy rose up, and still keeping his cock in her hand, turned her bottom to his belly and spitted herself on his prick, sitting straddled over his lap, a position that enabled her to enjoy the very last fraction of its length into her heated cunney. They stayed motionless as in a *tableau vivant* for a few moments, enjoying the mutual sensations of repletion and possession so delightful to each of the participants of an enjoyable fuck, before they commenced those soul-stirring movements that would lead inexorably to a grande finale of frenzy. One could almost feel their muscles contract and relax as she rocked up and down on his shaft.

As the orgasm approached she drove down hard with a delighted squeal, spearing herself on the luscious prick, which was now glistening from her cunt juice as they melted into a torrent of mutual spendings.

Nancy let Angus's limp tool slide out of her before she rolled over off him and the pair kissed passionately as Sir Jaspar led a round of applause.

'I wan't that impressed,' whispered Johnny. 'Sir Angus was very brief in foreplay before the actual fuck and Nancy didn't show off her attributes to full advantage. With a bum like hers, I think she should have gone for a bottom-fuck. I would love to have seen his thick shaft forcing its way between her chubby arse-cheeks into her cunt.'

'Yes, I think you are probably right,' I said, 'as very often a fuck from behind enables the clitty to be stimulated even more than when a shaft is fully enveloped from the front.'

'Shush, you two,' said Harold, 'I want to see the scores.'

The buzz of conversation quietened down as Sir Jaspar called for the judges to award their marks.

'May I please have your marks for style?' he called.

The three judges held up large cards which showed their verdict. In their right hands they held up cards with a single number upon them, and in their left hands they held up cards with fractions upon them.

Sir Jaspar bellowed out the marks: 'Six and a half, five and three-quarters, six and a quarter, which gives a total for style of eighteen and a half points.

'Now may I have your scores for entertainment? Thank you, gentlemen. Four and half, four and a half, four and a quarter, making an entertainment score of thirteen and a quarter points.

'And finally, will you award any bonus marks for fucking of especially high standard? Yes? No? Very well, an extra half mark from Mr Harknett Hughes giving Sir Angus and Nancy a grand total of thirty-two and a quarter points!'

The contestants bowed to the applause of the audience – did I mention that Albert Blair-Oliphant and the Countess

Estelle de Quenton and Professor Hugo de Sorrelle and Mrs Langtry were amonst the distinguished gathering? – and it was now the turn of the noted sportsman, Mr Wilson Brown and his paramour, Caroline Flistridge of Little Windmill Street, to take the stage.

The lights were dimmed and to our great pleasure, we found out that we were to be treated to an erotic entertainment of fucking with music. For as the couple, dressed in light blue satin robes held hands to begin their performance, all heads turned to the back of the room where three violins began to play a most beautiful melody. The musicians had slipped in unknown to all and I thought that the judges would certainly award extra marks for style to Wilson and Caroline.

'This is the first time I have heard music at a Victor Pudendum,' murmured Johnny. 'What is this lovely music?'

He was answered by Nathan Wabolowski. 'It is the *Adagio in G* by Albinoni,' he whispered, 'a most neglected composer who wrote more than fifty operas.'

I found the moving, emotional music perfectly suited to the slow, passionate embraces of the couple who were now tenderly in each other's arms lying on the mattress.

Wilson was a very good-looking young man. Indeed, he did not even look his age which was eighteen (as I was informed by Johnny later in the evening). He was tall and slim with curly fair hair, deep blue eyes, oh, he looked the very quintessence of boyish beauty. His nose was straight and is lips full and sensual. He was lucky enough to possess beautiful teeth and his smooth skin was like ivory. Indeed, if criticism could be made of his physical appearance it would be, I suppose, that he would have been thought a pretty girl if he had dressed himself in women's clothing!

As for Caroline, I must admit a twinge of jealousy for she too was a fine specimen of English womanhood. She too was just eighteen years old and showed no outward signs at least of the debauched life she had chosen for herself at the age of fifteen when she left the service of Sir Michael and Lady A--n-k. Sir Michael was well-known in Society for the robustness of his sexual powers but he was forced to throw Caroline out on the streets after his wife caught them in *flagrante delecto* after returning home unexpectedly. However, that old ram, Sir Michael, set her up in an apartment in Soho and since then she has wisely chosen her clientèle and is the proud owner of an account with Lazarus Freres worth over three thousand pounds.

But I digress, diary, forgive me. This beautiful brunette possessed a most bewitching expression of countenance with her large, full, dark eyes. Now Wilson was disrobing this gorgeous creature and there was an audible hiss of breath being sucked in as he revealed to us the firm swell of her lovely alabaster white breasts which he gently caressed, moving his hands over the large aureoles and raised nipples. He gently squeezed these succulent morsels up to a standing perfection whilst she shyly opened his robe to uncover his naked cock and balls. His cock was not fully erect as she slipped her hand around the glistening shaft but after a very brief moment, when Caroline rolled down the foreskin to expose the glistening, moist knob, his cock shot up ramrod straight under her touch.

They slipped out of their robes which were thoughtfully pulled off the mattress by Harold Le Meshigunah and to the liltingly sweet sounds of the violinists who stood some yards back behind us, they kissed and embraced as if they wished to lose themselves completely within the other – to let their senses be pervaded by the touch of skin, the sensual aroma of aroused passion . . .

Their gentle caresses rapidly acquired an urgency which she met with an equal display of desire. Then without a word they let go of each other. Caroline lay on her back arching herself like a sleek cat as Wilson knelt between her legs. He began to kiss her feet, her ankles, her calves and her knees and then as he started to kiss her inner thighs, his hands all the while massaging those divinely full breasts, she parted her legs as far as she could, fully exposing to us her luxuriant bush of silky brown hair and a pair of pink, pouting cunney lips between which jutted out a pert clitty just like a miniature cock! Wilson buried his head between her legs and we could hear (if not see) the boy suck deeply on her open cunney. I craned my head round to see him flick his tongue in and out between her cunney lips and then his hand came down from her titties to roll that erect clitty between a thumb and finger.

Perhaps it was the excitement of the music which was building up to a fine crescendo added to the superb champagne I had already consumed but my body was crying out with unfulfilled desire as Wilson continued to suck on and play with Caroline's cunt. Meanwhile, his proudly stiff prick was almost upright against his smooth, flat stomach. It irked me to see such a fine cock going begging, so to speak, and Johnny must have known what was in my mind as I stood up and began unbuttoning my blouse. He made no attempt to stop me, however, and in a short space of time I too was naked. I stood for a moment behind Wilson and admired his firm, manly buttocks. I turned around, however, facing the judges and slid under Wilson's parted knees – for he was still on all fours – so my head was just right under his hard cock. I grasped it in my hand, marvelling at the velvet smoothness of the skin that covered the iron-hard shaft. I kissed the shiny knob as I gave the shaft a gentle rub which seemed to make his prick swell up even further. I opened my mouth and took in as much of that delicious morsel as I could, eagerly sucking and lapping as I gently cupped his balls in my hand.

Wilson continued to bring Caroline off into new peaks of excitement with his tongue and out of the corner of my eyes I could see that she was spending love-juice which Wilson was eagerly licking up. She really had a gorgeous pouting cunt, which the poet must have had in mind when he penned:

Her bosom boasts no swell so fair
No tints that these eclipse;
Her head had no such auburn hair,
Nor such enchanting lips!

The attention he was giving to Caroline's cunt added to my lusty sucking of his prick was too much for any man to bear for long.

I felt Wilson's prick throb against my tongue and then woosh! His spunk pumped up the thick stem spilling warmly into my mouth.

But Wilson was a sexual athlete of great abilities! Even after I had greedily milked his lovely cock of the last drops of spunk, his prick remained rock-hard! Well, I was more than content to stay where I was, his stiff tool still in my mouth as I happily slurped away, nibbling at the juicy dome.

Now came a most unexpected occurrence. As I have already stated, Wilson's bottom was facing the judges and the sight of his lean, dimpled arse cheeks and wrinkled little bumhole proved too exciting not to a female member of the audience but to one of the judges! Yes, Mr Oscar Wilde, who Harold Le Meshigunah had mentioned as being a man of varied sexual proclivities, jumped up, pulled down his trousers and shouted: 'I must fuck that sweet boy!' And he promptly positioned himself behind Wilson and squeezed his cock (which fortunately was rather small) between Wilson's buttocks. With one hand Mr Wilde caressed that part of Wilson's shaft I could not jam into my mouth along with his balls, and with the other presented his prick to the tight little pink arsehole that kept bobbing towards him.

Wilson winced a little at the attack but Mr Wilde, being rather small, had no difficulty in effectually getting into him. 'Ooooh! Ooooh! how delicious,' panted Mr Wilde, 'I'm coming, I'm coming, I'm com –' and indeed he injected a copious emission into Wilson's bottom as the short convulsive jerks of his tool heralded a second squirt of frothy sperm which I eagerly swallowed, placing my tongue on the dome of his cock, rolling it over and over until even Wilson had to cry 'enough' and his cock began to lose its firmness.

Mr Wilde had also withdrawn his now flaccid prick from Wilson's bum and was busy pulling up his trousers. So far so good, and the musicians began to play a light piece, *What Are The Wild Waves Saying*, but Caroline made it plain that she remained unsatisfied. She stroked her moist cunney lips with her hands and ever the gentleman, Johnny was upon her, having thrown off his clothes in a madness of desire. He kissed the delicious girl with burning kisses and without ado, the purple dome of his prick was nudging between Caroline's cunney lips. She whimpered with pleasure and then Johnny arched upwards and thrust downwards, his hot cock spearing itself into her inviting pussey, penetrating deep into her womb, burying itself within the soft, luscious folds of her love sheath.

Caroline rolled over to her side and Johnny moved with her, not letting an inch of his cock out of her juicy crack. The girl's gorgeous bum was now exposed to view and Mr Wilde showed that he was a man for all seasons as yet again he pulled down his trousers but this time raised Caroline's beautiful rounded globes and inserted his stiff, short cock into her arsehole. She writhed with the pleasure and shock afforded by this new sensation and Johnny had to work hard to keep his prick inside her cunt. He must have been able to feel his cock rubbing against Mr Wilde's as only the thin divisional membrane was between them before with a cry, they jointly spent, deluging Caroline's cunt and bum with spurts of frothy spunk.

They collapsed in a heap as the music came to a stop and then roars of applause assailed my ears. I had been so caught up in this cornucopia of sensual activity that I had quite forgotten that the cream of London Society had not only seen me naked but also partaking of the lewdest of acts.

What would Aunt Portia say to me and later to papa and mama if word got out!

I flushed with embarrassment until Harold Le Meshigunah whispered to me: 'Well done, Jenny! Don't worry about anyone peaching about your little escapade. Many people here have secrets and they have all sworn on oath never to reveal what goes on in the Jim-Jam. Your secrets are as safe here as they would be in the Bank of England!'

Sir Jaspar Muttlebury called for silence to enable him to announce the marks awarded for the performance.

'My lords, ladies and gentlemen. I must inform you that the judges, with the greatest reluctance, have disqualified Mr Brown and Caroline from the contest.

'As many of you know, contestants must not be aided by outside helpers. However, as a token of our appreciation, we are awarding the young couple a certificate of distinction and a box at the Alhambra (courtesy of Signor Casati) for the new ballet *Irene*.'

I cheered this sporting gesture though I could not but feel a mite peeved as surely Johnny and I deserved a prize and I wanted to see *Irene*. All was well, though, as Wilson and Caroline later came round and insisted we joined them next week when they would take up the free pass issued by Signor Casati.

The contest was now at the half-way mark and proceedings were halted for a tasty light supper. We were served devilled chicken and a variety of sandwiches whilst the busy waiters forever hovered with more and more champagne. Mr Wilde came over to our table and congratulated me upon my participation in the *tableau vivant* (as he called it).

'I am rather inexperienced, I fear,' I said to the great man of letters.

'Do not distress yourself, Miss Everleigh,' he replied. 'Experience is what enables you to recognize a mistake when you make it again.'

'Well, be that as it may, at least Johnny and I will be able to see *Irene* at the Alhambra. It is supposed to be a most splendid ballet. Have you seen it, Mr Wilde?'

'Ah, yes, indeed, Miss Everleigh. I am sure that you will enjoy this latest terpsichorean wonder as much as I.'

'Is it worth taking a box?' inquired Harold Le Meshigunah as he fondly put his arm round Naomi, the pretty girl who was his partner for this extraordinary evening.

'Indeed it is, Monsieur Le Meshigunah. Suffice it to say that to recount the gorgeousness of scenery, costume and ballet would take longer than the few minutes we have before I return to my official duties. Perhaps we shall have a chance to talk after the programme has been completed.'

Sir Jaspar banged a gavel on the judges' table and called out that the Victor Pudendum contest would recommence in five minutes. Gradually, the audience drifted back to their seats, the lights were again dimmed and the next pair entered for the trophy were in place and ready to begin their performance.

Next in this sexual arena were the Honourable Cecil Knightley and Florence from 3, Golden Square, a well-known house of ill-repute although Florence was in fact a gifted amateur. She was a lady of independent means, her uncle being no less a personage than Major Soames Forsyte, but she enjoyed fucking so much that she preferred to spend an odd evening helping out Mr Alfred in Golden Square. Being a member of Society, she rarely condescended to fuck any man not found in Debrett's but was known to entertain good looking young men 'in trade' just occasionally.

Frankly, although both Florrie (as she was known to the cognoscenti) and Cecil were fine physical specimens, their performance was marred by an unfortunate spending too soon in the proceedings. But we did enjoy watching this fine pair for Cecil was a slim, handsome young man, his thick brown hair just a trifle long, his dark eyes smouldering with desire for the lovely girl who stood quite nude before him. Florrie was somewhat Rubensesque in build, of medium height with large breasts, wide expanding hips and rounded though firm buttocks.

In an inkling they were entwined on the bed, with Cecil's head ducking down beneath her ample thighs. She opened her legs wide as Cecil lifted up her hips and held her pussey against his mouth which we could hardly see as he sported a fine moustache. His tongue now thrust into her cunt as she cried out with joy. Cecil stabbed his tongue in and out whilst massaging her labia with his lips and his hands clutched handfuls of her plump bum cheeks. Now he was licking harder in slow but persistent strokes, kissing and sucking her cunney, rubbing his soft, moist lips against her cunt lips, mingling his saliva with her love juice which was already beginning to flow.

Florrie slid her fingers over her breasts, clutching and pinching her own nipples between thumb and finger. She closed her eyes and we could savour the waves of arousal that were rippling through her. Sensing perhaps that Florrie was too near the peak of passion, Cecil abruptly pulled his head back and turned her over face downwards on the bed. He grabbed a pillow and inserted it under her belly so that her hips and plump arsecheeks were raised up into the air. He moved between her legs, nudged her knees further apart, and taking his thick cock in his hand, capping and uncapping the purple helmet. He then carefully guided the head slowly into her dripping pussey from behind and began to fuck her in a slow yet steady rhythm. He was kneeling between her legs and bending forward so that his hairy chest brushed against her back. He reached under her and grabbed hold of her breasts, holding them in a firm grip as he continued to pump in and out of her juicy pussey.

Her plump bum slapped nicely against Cecil's thighs as she fitted easily into the rhythm he established, pounding away at her fleshy white bum. We relished the sight of his glistening cock see-sawing in and out of her cunney, above which the little brown wrinkled rosebud of her arsehole quivered and winked with each stroke. Reaching behind her, Florrie caressed his big balls with one hand as she rocked to and fro, her head thrown back and her hair whipping from side to side.

It was all too much for Cecil whose torso suddenly went rigid and his cock spurted spasm after spasm of spunk into her. His orgasm was so powerful that it seemed his body was being shaken to pieces as he gave a last drawn-out cry and collapsed on top of her, the perspiration pouring from him.

I felt sorry for Cecil who had obviously spent far too soon and even sorrier for Florrie who had enjoyed the joust but who had not achieved satisfaction. I would not have minded finishing the sweet girl off myself with my tongue and from the evidence of the bulge in their trousers, neither would have Johnny or Harold Le Meshigunah. But as our intervention had resulted in the disqualification of the previous pair, we felt constrained to keep our seats.

Cecil and Florrie retired to a round of sympathetic applause and after the judges had awarded their marks, we settled down to await the arrival of the last couple to try their luck in the Jim-Jam Victor Pudendum.

Now came the *pièce de résistance* – the final couple to take part in the contest entered the room and immediately I saw the handsome Negro I began to calculate my winnings! Remember, diary, that I had wagered three pounds at odds of eight to one!

The black man shucked off his robe and we ladies (and no doubt Mr Wilde) gasped in awe of his superb body. I think Joseph Hill must have had at least one European grandparent as his skin was of a light chocolate colouring whilst his features were quite finelly chiselled and his frizzy, curly hair was almost jet black. His physique was quite amazing – the muscles fairly rippled as he drew breath and expanded his magnificent chest. His torso narrowed down to a flat stomach and narrow hips and as he turned I admired his lean, muscular flanks. When he turned back I caught sight of his heavy, dangling shaft which was of a thickness I do not think I have seen before or since and my mouth watered just at the very thought of sucking that lovely prick up to full erection.

He was well matched by Nelly, one of the better girls to come from Great Windmill Street, who was rather slim, tall and dark with a beautiful plump rosy face, dark hair and dark, fiery eyes.

Nelly licked her lips and without wasting time reached down and encircled Joseph's fast-swelling black cock and I watched quite fascinated as she massaged it until it grew stiff and erect. He was now lying on the bed as she leaned over and took the pulsating, dark knob between her lips, jamming down the foreskin and lashing her tongue round the rigid shaft. Then she sucked hard, taking at least a third of this extraordinarily thick tool (which we later learned stood ten inches high though I never found out the measurements of its circumference) into her mouth while her hands played with his large, heavy balls.

Then she began to lick this monster prick, drawing her hot, wet tongue from his balls right up his shaft, flicking briefly at the gleaming knob. He clutched at her hair and shuddered as she circled her tongue all round the fleshy dome of his uncapped knob paying particular attention to the sensitive ridge. And then she removed her hands and clasping them behind her back she sucked up almost the entire length of his big cock almost down to the root and we could see Joseph twitch and jerk as Nelly sucked up and down his shaft with noisy abandon. This 'no hands' action brought a well-deserved round of applause from the audience.

She was obviously enjoying herself as now she had one hand in her own bush, rubbing her clitty as she continued to suck as much of that thick staff as possible, clamping her lips tightly around it.

By now I too was excited and my hand stole down

between my legs and I began to rub my own pussey which was deliciously damp. Johnny too was in a fine state of excitement and had taken out his not inconsiderable prick and was capping and uncapping the shining red head. For the sake of modesty I whispered fiercely that he should stop before someone saw him, so my bold young lover dived off his chair and placed his head under my skirt. And on his knees, he grabbed hold of my legs, pushing them apart against my feeble resistance and began to eat my pussey! I must have guessed this might happen as I was wearing no knickers, knowing how warm the atmosphere was likely to become!

Of course this meant that he was unable to see the rest of the performance. No man could resist the stimulation of having Nelly suck his cock in such expert fashion, and I could see that any moment she would be sucking up all the semen out of his hard, firm balls. Yes, Joseph had her head in his hands and was jamming her mouth down on his cock and those tell-tale quivers and convulsions began and she pushed up her head for a moment so we could see a great wash of white spunk come jetting out of the top of his prick. Nelly lapped up his jets of spunk and to my astonishment Joseph's prick remained as hard and strong as before he had climaxed!

Now it was Joseph's turn to take control and he leaned forward, his thick lips seeking and finding an engorged nipple that stood out like a tap ready to be drawn and he sucked first one and then the other nipple up to little peaks of glorious hardness. Nelly was now spread out flat on her back and she opened her legs wide, aching as I was, with Johnny flicking his tongue in and out of my pussey under the cover of my skirt, for a good stiff cock to slide into her cunt. She trembled and reached down to grasp the hard, throbbing shaft, guiding towards her oozing cunney. Joseph smiled and moved his head upwards to place his lips upon hers. She opened her mouth to take his tongue deep between her moist lips as Joseph stroked his cock slowly and then slipped his hand inside her cunney moving it in and out to widen the entrance for his tremendous prick.

Taking his cock in his left hand, he placed his knob at the opening of her cunt and pushed in and Nelly somehow succeeded in taking all his huge erection as I watched totally fascinated as I saw it disappear inch by inch inside her. Then he began to move it in and out in deep, gentle thrusts and I could hardly control my own moans as Johnny continued to slurp happily away at my pussey, rolling his tongue around my erect little clitty, bringing squirts of love-juice down upon his face.

Joseph began to attack again those saucer sized aureoles with those pert little nipples that just begged to be flicked by his long, tapering fingers. He then pulled right out of her, his black cock glistening with the juices from her pussey. Ever so lightly now his fingertips traced the open, wet slit of her cunt, flicking the erect little clitty that was peeping out. Then the cunney lips were forced apart as he took hold of his thick black pole and thrust the huge crown between the pouting lips of that juicy pussey and Nelly moaned again with delight as he propelled in inch after inch until his curly and her silky pubic hairs were matted together. He pulled back yet again and then drove the powerful length of his massive shaft full inside the lovely girl again and again as she urged him on, closing her feet together at the small of his back to force even more of that huge tool inside her. Joseph was now panting with exertion as he rammed his cock in and out of her cunt, his black body rocking backwards and forwards between her spread white thighs. Nelly was obviously spending as Joseph was fucking her as she raked his back with her fingernails as she savoured the voluptuous sensation of that big black cock in her voracious cunney. Joseph was now pumping faster and faster and people in the audience were now on their feet urging him onwards as at the very final stage he withdrew and shot floods of creamy white seed spurting all over her belly to an almost deafening roar of applause. Happily, Johnny brought me off beautifully just at the same time and he withdrew his head from under my skirt just in time to see Joseph spurt out his jets of spunk.

'Good heavens! The fella produces gallons of it!' he muttered.

'Never mind, darling,' I replied sweetly. 'Thank you so much for finishing me off with your tongue. I will repay the compliment as soon as we climb into the carriage to take us home!'

Well, to cut this long story short, Sir Jaspar announced that Joseph and Nelly were the winners of the trophy, a verdict that was greeted with universal approval and I was the proud possessor of twenty four sovereigns. Before we left I made my way to see Joseph Hill who was at the centre of a crowd of admiring girls. I managed to get him on one side and offered him ten of my golden coins.

'I think it only fair that you share my winnings as I wagered that you would win,' I said shyly.

He replied in a most beautifully modulated tone that if I had had my eyes shut would have convinced me that I was listening to a member of the House of Lords!

'That is most awfully generous of you, madam. Normally, I would not accept the gift but my kind master, Sir Heddon Court, has offered me the chance to take up a place at medical school here at University College. I was tutored at Court Lodge with Sir Heddon's eldest son Walter who will also study medicine there.'

I nodded and tried unsuccessfully to hide my surprise as Joseph continued in a gentle tone of voice: 'I am afraid that white people still cannot adjust to the fact that academic abilities are not confined to the Caucasians alone.'

I blushed with shame and nodded my agreement. [Dr Joseph Hill (1849–1936) was the first West Indian student to become a general practitioner in Britain. After working some years in the East End of London he emigrated to the United States where he established a hospital in Harlem in 1894 – Editor.]

So ended this exciting evening. True to my word I gobbled Johnny's cock in the darkness of the carriage on our way home thus giving the dear boy some much needed relief. Nathan Wabolowski and Harold Le Meshigunah stayed on with their girls at the Jim-Jam for a select private orgy organized by Professor Hugo de Sorrelle but I was too tired to participate. Poor Harold should also have left well alone as whilst he was fucking Naomi he had the misfortune to find Oscar Wilde up his arse and the poor man had to sit on soft cushions for three days afterwards. I thought this a shame but the news afforded Johnny a great deal of amusement.

October 16th, 1871

It is a bright autumn Sunday, diary, and I have all day to relax and note down in your pages more of the adventures that have befallen me since I arrived here in London just a few short months ago.

On Friday, Johnny and his friend Freddie Watson, an Old Harrovian, went down to Harrow to see the Goose Match, the last game of cricket played until the arrival of spring in all her glory.

The autumn has been quite mild this year and the lads enjoyed their game. Freddie was playing for the visitors' team which witnesses the great gathering of the cricketing clans. The match gets its name from the fact that the game continues until the players can see no longer and gas-lamps are lighted in the adjoining road. The rival teams then sit down to a bounteous repast and as soon as their digestions and the goose will best permit, retire to the Kings Head and fight over again the battles of their cricket lives.

Yesterday Freddie invited Johnny and I to the Watson's large town house in Old Brompton Road. We arrived separately as Johnny was playing football for the Old Foresters and would not be with us until after the match, which was against their old rivals the Old Citizens.

When I arrived, at about four o'clock, Freddie introduced me to his pretty girl friend, Maud, a real beauty who could best be described as a miniature of conventional English loveliness with gold-dusted light brown hair and soulfully expressive large brown eyes, who wore a low cut blue silk dress that revealed even as it covered the splendours of a pair of fully rounded breasts.

Freddie had obviously partaken of more than one, indeed more than two or three whiskies-and-soda for whilst we two girls sat rather primly in our chairs, he sprawled out on the sofa.

'Well, we have an hour or so until Johnny gets here,' he said. 'Why don't we play a game until he arrives?'

'Very well,' said Maud. 'What would you like to play darling?'

'How about forfeits?' I suggested.

'What a splendid idea,' said Freddie. 'Maud can set the question and I'll devise the forfeit!'

He reached out for a pencil and a sheet of paper on a side table and hastily scrawled down the forfeit.

'Are you both ready?' asked Maud. 'Here is the question and the person who answers incorrectly or is beaten to the correct answer by the other has to pay the forfeit.

'If it costs one penny to post a letter to Brighton which is fifty miles away, how much does it cost to post a letter to Bournemouth which is a distance of one hundred miles from London?'

'Tuppence!' shouted Freddie.

'No, no, you are too quick,' I retorted with a giggle. 'It costs one penny whether the letter has to travel one mile or one hundred!'

'Well done, Jenny!' cried Maud. 'As ever, your sagacity proves the superiority of the feminine sex. Freddie, dear, it is time for you to undertake your forfeit.'

'Oh no, I could not!' said Freddie. 'It would be too embarrassing!'

I snatched up the piece of paper from the table and read the contents out loud. 'Describe with frankness and with accuracy the details of your first sexual encounter. And this causes you embarrassment, Freddie? Pray, how would we ladies have felt if one of us had had to pay this due?'

'I'm sorry, Jenny,' he apologised. 'I'm afraid it was the whisky writing the forfeit.'

'No excuses are allowed,' I said sternly. 'Come on,

Freddie, Maud and I are not prudish. I would love to know how you first crossed the Rubicon.'

'So would I,' chirped up Maud. 'If I know you, Freddie, I would guess that you were only a lad when you discovered the pleasures of the flesh.'

'You really would like to hear how I lost my virginity?' he said, somewhat incredulously.

'Oh, yes, please!' we chorused.

'Very well,' he said. 'Here goes and I shall leave nothing to your imagination.' We settled down to hear his story, which I listened to attentively and took some notes so I can reproduce it quite faithfully, diary, in your pages.

'I was only sixteen years old and what I am about to describe happened during the Spring vacation. It was on a quiet evening after supper and I was alone in the house except for the servants. My parents had been invited to dine with Lord and Lady Trippelle who were holding a soiree – your friend Nathan Wabolowski was there, Jenny, along with that American pianist, Lane Wright, over whom all London was swooning that season. Anyhow, I had little to do and so I looked at my father's cabinet for a good novel. I had just finished Michael Pettie's "Tales of an Abacus" and was looking for another work of fiction when I espied this old book bound in green leather that I had never seen before tucked in behind a row of three volume novels.

'I pulled it out and to my surprise and delight found that it contained nothing but some very explicit coloured plates showing naked young men and women. The first section showed a young man having his stiff cock sucked off by a girl in a parlourmaid's uniform (something I had often imagined as I took my own prick in hand in the privacy of my own bedroom for Polly, our own chambermaid, was a comely wench not much older than I and I would have given a sovereign just to feel her lovely titties!)

'The pictures then proceeded to a time when the boy had shucked off his clothes and was about to place his cock into the yawning gap of the cunney that was there before him as the girl lay with her legs outstretched ready to receive him. I was entranced by this picture and my own hand stole down to my stiffening cock and I unbuttoned my trousers in order to grip my young pole. I was oblivious to the fact that none other than Polly had entered the room to take out any dirty ashtrays or filled wastepaper baskets.

'"My, my, Master Freddie," said this pert little vixen. "I do believe you have found your Papa's secret library!"

'"Yes, I most certainly have," I replied. "But how did you know about it, Polly?"

'"Ah, now that is the trouble with you fine ladies and gentlemen. You all go about your business thinking that your servants take nothing in. I could tell you a thing or two! Not about your parents, mind, but in my last situation, well, the master was fucking at least two of the maids as well as Signora Lagliani from the Italian Opera. Mind, I don't suppose you have had too much experience in that sort of way, Master Freddie, have you?"

'"N-n-n-no," I stuttered. "To be absolutely truthful, I haven't ever had the opportunity to, er, to, ah, to –"

'"To enjoy a good fuck, Master Freddie?" she said, her eyes all a-sparkle. "Why, I do believe you are still a virgin. Come now, admit it, there is nothing to be ashamed of in telling the truth."

'I hung my head in confusion and nodded my blushing assent to her query.

'Polly's eyes twinkled again, "Well, young man, wouldn't you like to do something about this sorry state of affairs? You look as if you are ready for your first fuck or have you stuffed a banana down the front of your trousers?"

'She smiled again and to my utter delight she set to work unhooking her dress and loosening the strings. She was a sprightly beauty well proportioned in leg and limb with a full swelling bosom and I gasped with admiration as she peeled off her underclothes to stand naked before me and I drank in the sight of the first nude girl I had ever seen – her large, uptilted breasts topped with those delicious cherry nipples, her flat stomach and down between her legs, a thatch of thick brown hair. In a trice, I was tearing off my clothes. Polly giggled deliciously as buttons popped as in my frenzy I tore the clothes from my body.

'"Don't rush so, Master Freddie," she laughed. "I haven't got a train to catch!"

'But my eager body drove me on and then, there, the last of my clothes were thrown off and I too stood naked before her! Alas, I was so nervous that my cock had shrivelled back almost to nothing. Fortunately, Polly was a sensitive creature and she knew all I needed was a little extra encouragement. So she dropped to her knees, rolled back my foreskin, took my soft cock in her hands and lapped at the uncovered dome. Rapidly my cock began to swell under her kind ministrations and I instinctively moved forward to push my hardening prick into her mouth. Her magic tongue circled my knob, savouring the juices and her teeth scraped the tender flesh of the underside as she drew me in between those luscious lips, sucking slowly from base to top and back again, delighting me to hitherto unknown peaks of sensual pleasure. I was overcome with the ecstasy of the moment and when Polly began to handle my balls at the same time, it was too much for my impatient prick and the rush of excitement surged through my body and I filled her mouth with spurts of boiling spunk which is exactly what she had wanted. She eagerly swallowed my emission and gurgled with joy to see that my young cock was at least semi-erect even after discharging its load of love-juice.

'"Now you may fuck me," she whispered, laying herself down on the rich Turkish carpet. "I will just give your cock a little rub to make it hard again and then you can pop it in my pussey."

'Again, I viewed with delight the narrow triangle of bushy brown hair that hid her cunt. But then she parted her legs and stroked her delicate little cunney, motioning me to put my hand there too. I needed no second invitation and felt for the soft, warm lips of her pouting pussey which moistened at my touch. "That's right, Freddie, suck them nicely," she said softly as my head sank to her breasts and I began to lick at an aroused red tittie. I continued to explore the hairy tuft between her legs and the divine girl opened her legs wider to let my finger slip further inside her juicy notch.

'"Now, Freddie, now, stick your lovely cock inside me! I want it all, oh, Freddie, please fuck me!" I pushed my prick towards the glistening red lips but could not effect an entrance in my hurried frenzy. So the kind girl took hold of my throbbing tool and guided it herself, inserting the uncapped dome into the welcoming folds of her cunney. Polly possessed a marvellous gift of contracting her pussey so that it took hold of my cock like a delicate soft hand frigging the shaft and she wriggled away as I pumped my raging prick in and out of her sodden cunt, her vaginal muscles caressing my cock as we went faster and faster, and she bucked and twisted, urging me to thrust deeper, deeper as she raised her legs and wrapped them behind my shoulders. How tightly her cunt enclasped and sucked upon my prick and we gloried in each giant thrust as her love-juices dropped upon my balls as they banged against her arse. Cupped now in my broad palms, her tight bottom cheeks rotated almost savagely as my lusty cock rammed in and out. Her kisses now rained upon my neck whilst the friction in her cunt reached new heights.

'It was too exciting to last and arching my body upwards, I plunged down hard, crushing her springy breasts beneath me as her legs flexed and my frothy seed poured into her pulsating pussey as I pushed in, pushed away, pushed in and back again as her clever cunney milked my prick of every last drop of spend pumping my fluids out into her dark, secret warmth.

'Oh, the joy of that wonderful first fuck. I shall never forget that lusty deflowering until my dying day. This was a stepping stone into adulthood that could have been a traumatic experience. First love can often be disastrous for both partners. I was most fortunate to enjoy tuition from a dear, sweet girl who overcame my naivity and made my first journey down the highway of love such an exhilarating journey!'

We listened spellbound to Freddie's frank and fluent narration and spontaneously, Maud and I broke into a round of applause.

'I did enjoy hearing how you crossed the sexual Rubicon,' I said. 'My only regret is that you have made me feel quite randy and I must wait now until Johnny returns from his football and has his tea before I can quench this thirst!'

'I'm sure Maud won't mind if I attend to the needs of an honoured guest,' laughed Freddie, 'although I am not sure that my cock is as big as Johnny's.'

'Oh, you men have a fixation about your cocks!' cried Maud. 'How many times must I tell you that size hardly matters – it is what you do with your equipment that matters so very much more!'

I nodded my agreement but could hardly keep my eyes from the tell-tale bulge that had developed in the crotch of Freddie's trousers.

'Anyway, have I ever complained about the dimensions of your prick?' asked Maud with some heat. 'Really, Freddie, you should know better. Would you like to have a look at it, dear Jenny, and then perhaps you can reassure Freddie that he has nothing at all to worry about?'

'Certainly, I would be only too happy to oblige,' I replied and together we made a dive for Freddie's lap. Maud unbuttoned his fly whilst I extracted a not inconsiderable cock, which grew in my hand as I tickled it and I bent down and sucked up a bead of translucent ooze that had already poured from its tip.

We pulled his trousers and underpants off and Maud licked her lips as she saw that his prick was ready for action. She unhooked her skirt and took off her own undergarments so that she too was ready for a little joust and then she positioned herself above Freddie, wanting to sit on him and ride a St George. Ever willing to help, I took hold of his throbbing prick, uncapped the purple dome and planted it firmly between the moist, gaping little hole between Maud's pussey lips. I watched his shaft disappear upwards into her willing cunney and as she began to bounce up and down upon Freddie, my own hand stole under my dress to play with my own aching pussey. Oh, would Johnny never return from his stupid game?

Freddie clasped his arms around her, taking one globe of her bosom in each hand which he moulded delightfully as she rose and fell on his tight-fitting shaft, and Maud leaned forward to meet his kisses and give him her tongue in his mouth. This was obviously a position that both favoured for I have rarely seen a more voluptuous engagement that was so enjoyed by both partners. Freddie spent and lay still for a few moments but then, with an upward motion of her buttocks, Maud challenged him to go on and after his recovery the lucky lad spent fifteen minutes more on his back before he shot a second spurt of spunk into Maud's insatiable womb.

After they had recovered, we washed and refreshed ourselves for the servants would soon be coming in to lay out our tea. And indeed, the tea trolley had just been wheeled in when Johnny arrived, sporting an enormous bandage around the shin of his left leg.

'Hallo, everyone!' he said, limping heavily as he came towards me for a kiss. 'I am so sorry that I am late but unfortunately I took a rather nasty kick on the shin and Doctor Burbeck insisted on cleaning it up and putting on this bandage.'

'Does it hurt very much, darling?' I inquired.

'It's not too bad, though I did hit the roof when the good doctor put some iodine on the cut.'

'But how did it happen? I thought you were playing Association rules?' said Freddie.

'Yes, that's right, I prefer Association to the Rugby code, but in fact, it was all a complete accident. Lord Kinnaird crossed a perfect ball from the left wing and the ball bounced in front of me. At the same time, one of the Old Citizen defenders, young Nick Sayers, you know him, the chap that almost bankrupted the bookies at Goodwood last year when he backed four successive winners, swung his leg and quite by accident caught me a beauty. He was most apologetic and insisted that I let him know how the wound progresses. No bones broken though, according to Doctor Burbeck, so let's not make too much fuss about it!' insisted my brave lover who despite his words was surely in no little discomfort.

'I think football should be banned. It is no game for gentlemen,' said Maud. 'One reads all the time of the large number of accidents and I have seen severe comments about the game not only in the ordinary newspapers but in the medical journals.'

'Hold on a moment,' said Freddie. 'The same enquiry would be equally pertinent with regard to many of the most popular of our sports, especially to those where physical skill and dexterity contribute so much towards success. Hunting and shooting have their elements of danger –'

'And so does cricket as Jenny can testify,' added Johnny.

'Yes, indeed,' Freddie continued, 'each sport has its risks and might be held responsible, in particular degree, to public opinion. Accidents, and of a fatal character, are not unknown in any of them; and indeed some kindred sports would, I am inclined to think, hardly have made the best of a comparison if a fair and impartial analysis were made of their respective dangers.'

'You must pardon me, but I have to take issue with you on this subject,' said Maud, who was (as I should previously have mentioned) studying nursing at London University. 'Why, only recently I heard Professor Schmocke declare that there was hardly a match of any importance at which an accident more or less serious did not occur.'

'My dear Maud, of course there is a certain amount of bodily risk,' said Johnny with some exasperation creeping into his voice. 'In any game where personal contact is inevitable there must naturally be some chance of physical injury especially where enthusiasm runs, as is frequently the case, very high. And in any case, any estimate of the risks of football would be quite unfair when the high number of players who regularly follow the game as a source of recreation and excercise is not fully taken into account. And I might add that I have played football every winter since the age of fifteen and have never seen a serious accident.'

'Well, perhaps I have exaggerated the dangers,' admitted Maud. 'Yet I still believe that public opinion is entitled to claim that any amusement that is calculated to be of detriment to the youth of this country should be rigorously supervised.'

'I would not disagree with you there,' replied Johnny. 'But ask yourself, would football ever have reached its present popularity had there not been a strong and general feeling that it was a manly game, tending to exercise, and to a marked degree, many of the faculties which have contributed so much to the success of the Anglo-Saxon race? Football has done much to mould and fashion the character for endurance and enterprise which has come to be one of the recognized qualities of an Englishman.

'It gives opportunities for healthy and stimulating exercise at a time of year when brisk and invigorating motion is essential to warm the body and allow free circulation of the blood. It inculcates habits in youth which cannot fail to be of use in later life – pluck, energy, the abnegation of self for the common good, decision of mind to utilize in an emergency. And for our humbler sons of toil, has not football offered to thousands of working men a harmless relaxation away from the enervating atmosphere of the public house? It would not be difficult to demonstrate the benefits which football, week after week, confers on thousands of the hardest working members of the community. Its popularity is increasing and will surely spread overseas, though personally I can never see any foreigners being able to play as well as the English – except of course from the Empire!'

'You don't think the Europeans could ever take up football?' I asked. 'Really, Johnny, you are such a bigoted chauvinist.'

'No, I strenuously deny the charge,' he replied earnestly. 'But the thought, say, of Italy taking on England at football is laughable, Jenny. Why, you might as well expect the South American dagoes to give us a game!' (Johnny Oaklands (1851–1913) played for the Old Carthusians and later was a Vice President of the Casuals who toured Europe during the early years of the twentieth century. He lived to see soccer catch on in Europe but not among the 'dagoes' mentioned here – Editor)

'What are we arguing about, anyway?' interrupted Freddie. 'Come on, I'm starving, let's tuck in to tea.'

'I'll take charge,' said Maud, a little miffed about being worsted in her argument with Johnny. 'Who would like cake and who bread-and-butter?'

After we had eaten a substantial tea Freddie opened three bottles of a very drinkable claret and I'm forced to admit, a little sexual horesplay took place.

We had all gone upstairs to Freddie's bedroom to look at the fancy dress costumes he and Maud were going to wear that night at the Bloomsbury Ball given by Sir Louis Baum in aid of Distressed Widows and Dependents of The London Bookselling Trade. Freddie was attending as Napoleon Bonaparte and Maud as the Empress Josephine. The costumes were amonst the finest Aspiso (the firm who provided most of the clothes worn at Colonel Norbert's ball which, diary, I described earlier in these recollections) could provide and I must say they looked very splendid just hanging up on the door of Freddie's wardrobe.

'I think I will try my dress on now, Freddie,' said Maud who was slightly the worse for wear under the influence of her fourth glass of claret. 'You men leave the room whilst Jenny assists me in dressing off my take. No, I mean offing dress my take, no I don't, I mean, taking off my dress. There, that's right, just be good boys, please.'

Johnny and Freddie moved reluctantly to the door but I shooed them through and closed the door behind me. 'Do you need any help, Maud?' I asked.

'No, not really,' she said, a little more briskly than before. 'I'm not really sloshed but I just wanted to get rid of the boys for a little. I hope you don't mind too much.'

'Not really,' I said. 'What have you in mind, Maud?'

'I am feeling rather horny, Jenny,' she confided. 'But unfortunately Freddie has run out of French letters and I dare not have a cock up my cunt at this time or I would be in danger of having my belly swell up. I have two lovely dildoes in the bag you will find under the bed and I would be most grateful if you would join me in a mutual fuck.'

'But of course!' I cried. 'It is always a pleasure to help a sister in distress. Now, where are the dildoes?'

I reached down and pulled out a brown paper bag from under the bed. I fumbled inside and took out two beautifully made dildoes, made of the finest india rubber and fashioned absolutely faithfully to look and feel just like a fully erect cock.

I began to undress as quickly as I could leaving Maud to pull down my bloomers to reveal my blonde thatch of pubic hair. She ran her finger along the length of my slit, allowing it to come to rest at the base of my clitoris. She then grasped my bum cheeks, one in each hand, and gently kissed my moistening pussey, her mouth pressed against the soft, yielding flesh, probing gently with her tongue.

Soon we were entwined together in a *soixante neuf*, Maud's head buried between my legs whilst my busy fingers were busy, nipping and pinching her own finely developed clitty. Then I pulled her pussey to my own lips and nuzzled them round the curly bush that surrounded her cunt. Maud wriggled and cooed with delight as she grabbed hold of a dildo and passed it, with a little giggle, across to me. I took hold of the affair and pressed it to her wet cunney lips and I must confess that I found the thrusting of the dildo in and out of her sopping cunney quite exciting. Wildly she began to peak, twisting and writhing as I plunged the dildo in and out of her insatiable cunney. Her fingers slipped juicily in and out of my nether lips and my own orgasm came rushing at me quickly, taking my outer edges first, moving in waves towards my centre and shuddering I spent profusely on her fingers. She then wriggled over on her tummy and stuck her firm bum cheeks up in the air, slightly parting her legs so that I had full view of the tight-looking wrinkled brown hole between the glorious cheeks of her bum. I attacked the fortress with vigour, dipping the rubber cock in and out of the puckered rosette as Maud cried out: 'Ah, Ah, Ah, you'll rend me but no, no, don't stop! Oh, Oh, Oh, Ah! you're there!' I continued to fuck her arsehole with the dildo and I could see from the wrigglings of her rounded bum cheeks that she was enjoying it. My other hand was kept busy frigging her sopping cunt in front. She shuddered to a sublime peak and there followed the juicy sounds of love, a chorus of ecstatic sighs and squeals as we continued to pleasure ourselves to a state of exhaustion.

Our cries of delight were heard by the boys as they came tumbling in to find me on my back with my legs spread wide and Maud's eager face between them lapping furiously away at my pussey.

'Gosh, just look at those two tribades!' cried Freddie as I wrapped my thighs round Maud's neck, locking her head deliciously in my gushing grotto.

'I think we should show them what their cunts are really made for,' grinned Johnny, his hands already unlocking his belt. 'Come on, Freddie, old chum let's give the girls a jolly good fucking!'

Ever the gentleman, Freddie first enquired as to whether this was what we wanted. 'I would never presume to insert my cock in a cunt that did not wish it to be there!' he said, drawing himself up to his full height.

'No, don't worry, darling,' said Maud, lifting up her face from my sopping muff, 'but you may only fuck my bumhole as it is the time of the month when I could get pregnant which would be deucedly awkward for us both!'

Without wasting time, the boys stripped naked and Johnny positoned himself just behind my head, kneeling so that his nicely stiff cock stood out just above my nose. Maud looked up to see this juicy cock in front of her and, to my great annoyance, she stopped sucking my clitty to suck the helmet of Johnny's cock into her mouth. I could see her relish the purple domed morsel as she licked away voraciously as I saw Freddie anoint his fingers with some cold cream which he rubbed on his bursting, swollen purple helmet. He then carefully positioned the head of his cock between Maud's bum cheeks and opening them apart, inserted his creamed cock into her wrinkled rosette, which had fortunately just been stretched by the rubber dildo.

'Ooooh! Ooooh!' she gurgled, still sucking away on Johnny's meaty shaft as Freddie found his way in, rested a moment and then slowly began his fucking motions, burying his shaft up to the hilt as his balls flopped against Maud's heaving buttocks. Freddie had corked her to the limit as he moved in and out in a slow shunting movement as his right hand snaked round her waist to join my hands in exploring her engorged cunney. Lucky Maud! As I massaged her erect little clitty, Johnny spunked jets of frothy cum into her mouth as she worked her bum to bring off Freddie who flooded her bumhole with jets of juice. This brought Maud up to a second delicious spend and shortly afterwards, with a 'pop', Freddie uncorked his still stiff cock from her well lubricated arsehole.

I was glad that my three companions had enjoyed themselves so heartily. The boys had shot their loads and Maud had achieved a vibrant orgasm but here was I, totally out of the game and feeling distinctly out of sorts.

Johnny must have sensed my mood as he looked lasciviously at my large breasts that stood up firmly as he gave them a loving squeeze. Then he took hold of one of the rubber dildoes and guided it over the hills and valleys of my breasts. Round and round it went tickling my titties till they stood rock hard. My body arched with exquisite pleasure as spasm after spasm ripped through me. Johnny leaped on top of me and plunged the dildo into my sopping pussey. His thick prick was staring me in the face and it was already wet as I took it gently into my mouth, sucking hard as the dildo teased round my clitty and I eased his lovely cock out of my mouth and placed it between my cunney lips where it belonged! This excited Maud and whilst Johnny banged his cock in and out of my juicy cunt, she played with herself using the second dildo whilst Johnny ran his rubber prick up and down the cleavage of my tight little bum. The penetrating pulsations of cock and dildo really excited me, creating a wild sexual ecstacy. A dildo and a cock together certainly give a girl a feeling that she will never forget!

My pleasure was now heightened by Freddie who knelt by my side and of course his cock was standing at attention waiting for me to turn my head and suck it. I closed my fingers around it and began to tease it with my tongue, pulling back the foreskin and licking the pink knob-end, savouring the salty, sensuality of its taste. He thrust his slippery prick deeper into my mouth as I helped him by slipping my lips as far down the shaft as they would go, feeling his wiry pubic hair tickling my nose as I inhaled its perspiring fragrance. He spent quickly with a low moan as I swallowed his spunk gratefully, pulling him hard into me as he delivered the contents of his massive balls deep in my mouth. I sucked on his still stiff cock until the last drops had been given to me.

I could still feel Johnny's stiff thickness inside me and he gave me great joy by moving firmly in and out of my cunt, achieving maximum penetration with his cock whilst presenting the head of the flexible rubber dildo to my bumhole. I caressed his head and we kissed passionately as my approaching climax made me gasp out involuntary noises of pleasure. Then I knew that his climax too was nigh and he jumped and bucked inside me as his prick shot warm balm into my sopping cunney. It was a splendid fuck. Never shall I forget the thrill as Johnny drove that lovely bone-hard tool into my aching womb. We enjoyed a superb mutual spend and we lay panting with lustful exhaustion.

We continued to fuck each other for another hour or so but then we had to say *au revoir* as we went our separate ways – Maud and Freddie to their ball and Johnny and I to dine at Lord and Lady Dartie's imposing mansion in the heart of Belgravia. I'm afraid that neither Johnny nor I were at our best at the dinner table as we were both so tired from our afternoon's fucking and besides Johnny's football injury was hurting him quite badly.

But we stayed until a time when it could not be considered rude to leave and I spent the night with Johnny in Albion Square. We were so exhausted that I could have truthfully told Aunt Portia that I had slept alone! But we made up for the barren night with a glorious fuck before breakfast the next morning!

October 28th, 1871

Season of mists and mellow fruitfulness!
Close bosom-friend of the maturing sun;
Conspiring with him how to load and bless
With fruit the vines that round the thatch-eaves run;

John Keats' *Ode to Autumn* has long been one of my favourite poems, perhaps because of all the seasons I enjoy autumn best. I wandered happily the other day through Kensington Gardens and on a fine if somewhat chill morning it was good to hear the first thrushes singing. Starlings were swarming around the garden's crab-apple trees pecking wastefully at the bright red fruit. Leaves were still to be found lingering in some trees – deep shiny yellow on the birches, pale green and yellow on the elms. I strolled along lazily, kicking away the leaves that were scattered along the damp ground.

I have begun this entry, dear diary, with the words of Keats but in truth my thoughts that crisp morning were on an entry of a different kind. Johnny had been summoned to visit his Uncle Silas who was the titular head of the Oaklands clan. There was some trifling legal matter to be discussed which required Johnny's attendance and I had been invited to dine with his old friend Ronald. Now although Johnny is not the jealous type and though and perhaps because of this I love him very dearly, I do have this constant urge to fuck good-looking young men. Ronald was not handsome in the classical style but I was attracted to the thick black hair that curled all over his head, from his low forehead to the back of his neck. His head is of a good shape, full and round, broad over the brows and high above the orifice of the ear.

His eyes are brown and not over large but well set, and his nose is slightly aquiline, while his delicate black moustache showed the pleasant curve of his even lips. There was a fine colour in his cheeks too – that rich colour that dark men often possess in their youth.

You may rightly judge, diary, that after a delicious if somewhat spicy meal at which I imbibed an over abundance of champagne, I was unresisting when Ronald joined me on the sofa and kissed me passionately on the mouth. I made no protest when his tongue flickered into my mouth nor when his hands scooped out my proud breasts from my gown. He really knew how to excite my sensual senses and I needed little persuasion to feel the hard protuberance that bulged out the crotch of his trousers.

He moved his mouth downwards, sucking an elongated nipple into his mouth while his teeth nibbled the sensitive tip, sending waves of desire shooting through my groin. Then his hands moved upwards, searching underneath my dress and gently he parted the soft flesh of my thighs, found the waistband of my drawers and pulled them down to my feet. I wriggled as I could feel the pussey juice oozing out of me as his hand returned to travel through my thick brush of cunney hair for the soft, moist cleft and its guardian love button. As we continued to fondle each other he pushed his fingers down and in, sliding through my wetness and I began to moan, feeling my hips rotate. Oh, how naughty I was to let Ronald diddle me but he did it so nicely, stroking up the side of my clitty then down again, letting a finger slip right into my pussey then rubbing the juices up and down again.

I looked into his lap and my fingers opened up his fly buttons to release his bursting cock that leaped and bounded like a tube of hard, yet velvety ivory as I moved my hand slowly up and down the shaft.

We were now well past any point of return as Ronald thrust my legs apart and raised himself above me. I let go his prick to raise my dress as I lay down and Ronald roughly ripped away my drawers from my ankles. He placed his enormous cock against my slit and I felt the huge bulb press into my wetness. For a second or two our hot eyes locked together and then with a cry of joy he inserted three inches of his meaty shaft and was full upon me. We rocked to and fro as I wriggled my bum to obtain more of his cock. I wanted to be filled with his marvellous prick, which was not so huge in length but of such a thickness and so good to be fucked with! I could feel its fat, gleaming head stretching my cunt which in some magical way expanded to receive it.

Again and again, he pounded in and out, faster and faster at the most fantastic speed which I could not even attempt to match. I gloried in each powerful stroke as my love juice coated his cock making it slide even more freely. I implored his tongue the more by twirling my own in his mouth as I felt the ecstatic pleasure building up inside me. We were now locked into that world where fulfilment is all and my body was racked with uncontrollable spasms as delicious waves of pleasure spread outward from my womb like ripples on a lake.

'Ah! Oh! Oh! I spend! Oh, what ecstasy! Ah! heavens what bliss!' I screamed out, almost fainting from excess of emotion as Ronald's body went rigid as he shot a torrent of gushing seed into me. He rolled off me, gasping for breath, and though we would have both enjoyed a continuation, the champagne was now taking its toll and we fell into the arms of Morpheus almost immediately.

Ronald woke me up at midnight and we decided that for the sake of Johnny's pride (and of Ronald's pretty fiancee!) we would not repeat a performance of that night's joys. It was such fun though, I mused, scrunching the wet leaves under my feet. But was it an experience I should care to repeat? Ah well, experience is what enables us to recognize our mistakes when we repeat them!

My reverie was interrupted by a man's voice calling out: 'Miss Everleigh, Miss Everleigh, Jenny, it is you, isn't it?'

The voice was familiar and I looked behind me to see

none other than our old friend Harold Le Meshigunah standing some fifty yards away.

'Jenny Everleigh,' he called out, 'I thought it was you walking alone so intently through the wood. You look as though there may be something on your mind. I hope young Johnny is playing the game fair and square?'

I blushed as I recalled what had just been passing through my mind. 'It is kind of you to inquire,' I said, 'but Johnny is not in my bad books. He is away actually at his Uncle Silas's house. Indeed, I am surprised that you are not there, Harold, as I believe the Oaklands family are having a big discussion as to their financial affairs.'

'Yes, or course that is where Johnny may be found,' laughed Harold. 'Of course the whole Oaklands clan are there debating how they can engineer more money from me, the damned foreigner, you know who keeps them all in the style to which they are accustomed.'

'Don't they accept you even after all your kindnesses?' I asked.

'Not really, Jenny,' said Harold. 'The English upper classes stick closely together and admit few strangers to their fraternity. It hardly bothers me though as I don't think that I should want to join any club that would accept me as a member!'

I smiled at him and said, 'Well I know how good you are to Johnny. I don't see why you should keep the whole family just because you married into it.'

'I am exaggerating,' said Harold, 'I have rescued them a couple of times from spectacularly bad investments. Any rogue could chisel money from that crowd. The trouble is, Jenny, that they are both greedy and lazy. They don't want to work and demean themselves by going into trade yet they expect huge returns on their investments.

'Just to give you an example, Jenny, a few months back some charletan sent a letter to Johnny's father offering him twenty-five per cent on any money invested in his company. He followed this up with a visit to the house and plausible though he was, it should have been obvious to anyone with a grain of common sense that no one can offer such a high rate of return without a considerable risk attached. I mean, I might ask you to invest in my skill at the roulette table or upon the racecourse. It is just possible that my luck will hold and I will be able to even double your investment – but the odds are against it.

'Believe me, dear Jenny, anyone not versed in financial affairs is best advised to take advice from one's solicitor, bank manager or accountant. If only the Oaklands family would learn this simple lesson!'

'I am sure you are right,' I said as we strolled together towards the gate. 'Johnny always tells me that you give him the most sensible advice.'

'Where are you going now?' said Harold. 'I have a little free time as I am waiting for my good friend Doctor David Lezaine to arrive from Brussels.'

'He is a compatriot?' I asked.

'Yes, he is a Belgian like myself. But Doctor Lezaine is a specialist on, how do you say it in English, on intimate affairs.'

'On intimate affairs?' I queried.

'Yes, Jenny, you know, on intimate matters between men and women.'

'Oh, you mean on fucking, Harold. Don't be shy, you may speak bluntly to me.'

'Well, thank you, but I do not like to use English colloquialisms often as I am unsure as to whether they offend.'

'Better to be safe than sorry,' I advised. 'Although I must say how strange it is how some harmless little words cause such great offence.'

'Yes, one must be very careful. For instance, my wife hates the word "cunt".'

'Many women do,' I explained, 'although the word has been in use since the Middle Ages. I believe it is of Teutonic derivation and means wedge. It is a vulgarism although

Chaucer used it in the Canterbury Tales, and cunt is a word many men use in speech although never to ladies. I do not understand why it should be so but many women feel that the word is hostile to the feminine sex.

'Funnily enough, this is not true of the converse case, for words such a "prick" or "cock" do not contain any aggressive or degrading connotations. It is a curiosity of the English language,' I added.

'Or a curiosity of the English male psyche,' smiled Harold, 'although my old friend Doctor Lezaine is better qualified to pronounce upon the matter. If you are free, Jenny, perhaps you would like to meet David, who will be at Victoria at noon. I think you will find him an interesting man to talk to though I must warn you now that he has a fearsome reputation amongst the ladies of Brussels.'

'Is he unmarried?'

'No, he has a wife and family but his wife's family live in Monte Carlo and Marlene is always taking the children down there for long breaks whilst David travels the world. You do not have to worry about language as he speaks three languages fluently, Flemish, French, and English, although Johnny says he speaks four.'

'Four?'

'Yes, Flemish, French, English and rubbish! Mind, this was when Johnny consulted him about a wart on his penis. David told Johnny that warts can be passed on to sexual partners and that he should refrain from fucking for at least six weeks. In fact, as David predicted, the wart went away of its own accord though I have doubts as whether Johnny listened to the wise advice he was given.

'Anyhow, David is coming here to undertake research at the University College in Bloomsbury. He is currently engaged in the writing of a book that will show how foolish our present age is regarding such affairs. The idea, for instance, that a woman partakes of sexual intercourse as a duty and not a pleasure is very much a product of our own benighted age.'

'I would like to meet Doctor Lezaine,' I said, 'so long as I will not be in the way.'

'Far from it, Jenny. We will have to eat a quick luncheon as David is lecturing to the medical students who have signed up for his course as he is giving some lectures in exchange for the facilities being afforded him by the college.'

Harold's carriage was waiting for us and we trotted round to Aunt Portia's to take morning coffee after our enjoyable constitutional.

What a commotion there was at Victoria although we arrived there in good time. The Boat Train was only three minutes late and it disgorged a huge number of passengers. We had not long to wait though before Harold spied his friend.

'David, David, *nous sommes ici*,' he cried out and I caught sight of Doctor Lezaine as he turned to face us.

Doctor Lezaine cut quite an imposing figure. He was a tall, bulky man with merry eyes and a black goatee beard flecked with grey. He was wearing an Inverness cape and looked so smartly dressed even after the long journey. I have often noticed that Continental men appear more dapper than the English variety. Mind, the most elegantly dressed man I know is John Gibson, a Scottish friend of the family to whom we repair when we travel North of the Border, and there lies another story to be told in a later edition of these annals.

He waved his walking stick at us and the two men embraced in the Continental style, kissing each other's cheeks, again a habit that I find quite agreeable but is looked upon with scorn by some of the more insular of our countrymen.

He must have tipped the porter generously as the man took great care in unloading the cases from the wheelbarrow and piled them neatly upon the ground beside us and Harold leaned against them whilst we awaited the arrival of our carriage.

Doctor Lezaine, or David as he insisted upon my calling

him after we had effected our introductions, must have been at least forty-five years of age but he soon showed us that his sense of sight and reflexes of action were still of the highest quality.

For, as ever, there was a fearful amount of vehicular traffic and King, the coachman, had been forced to let us alight and move the carriage on to Grosvenor Gardens, taking strict instructions to return in fifteen minutes. Since our new friend had arrived so promptly, we were now waiting for King to bring the carriage round. And whilst we stood there a good-looking and well-dressed man of about thirty years of age, having the appearance of a smart man of business, stood next to Harold, apparently also waiting for the arrival of his conveyance. In the meantime, crowds of people passed to and fro and hordes of cabs, carts and omnibuses rumbled by.

I certainly had not noticed the stranger's left hand dropping by his side in the direction of my pocket. But Doctor Lezaine had noticed it glide in the direction of the pocket in my skirt, which as it happened contained nothing but a lace handkerchief though the would-be thief of course had no knowledge of what was to be found, and was about to plunge his hand in to extract whatever was inside, when David instinctively hooked his wrist with the curve of his walking stick and prevented the robbery.

'Ow!' said the thief, withdrawing his hand, and twisted away to try and run away. He was prevented from doing so however by David's leg which he stuck out to trip up our pickpocket.

Harold hauled the man up and said: 'That would have been a mean theft, my man. You look healthy enough, why cannot you obtain gainful employment? Frankly, you are not even a good pickpocket!'

'Forgive me gentlemen, and you too my lady,' he cried. 'I am not by nature a common criminal but I am driven by force of necessity to beg or steal for my livelihood.'

'A likely tale,' said Harold. 'You are only saying that so

we will let you go and refrain from calling a constable to have you arrested.'

'No, no, that is not true,' he said vigorously and turning to me he said: 'My lady, I do beg your pardon for attempting to rob you. Please forgive me.'

'I forgive you,' I said, 'if you will tell us what fate has driven you to such a foolish course of action.'

'I do not think I could, ma'am,' he said. 'It is a wretched tale not fit for the ears of a high-born lady such as yourself. For a start it involves delicate affairs about which I doubt would even make sense to you.' And saying that, the poor fellow fell down in a swoon though fortunately Harold broke his fall by supporting his shoulders as he slumped backwards.

At this juncture King brought up the carriage and as the coachman bundled David's cases onto the vehicle, we decided to take the thief with us.

'Where are you taking me?' he said as he regained consciousness.

'That depends,' said Harold carefully. 'I think your destination lies in whether you are in deserving need of aid. For a start, why did you faint just now? Was it an excess of emotion?'

'No, sir,' he replied. 'It was probably because I have not eaten since the evening before last for despite my smart dress, I am now desperately poor and I have no knowledge as to where my next meal is coming from.'

'Well I do,' said David decidedly. 'You can have something to eat at my club when we arrive there. If we ever arrive, I should say. *Ma foi*, Jenny, your London traffic grows more congested every time I visit the city. I sometimes think you should knock down most of London and build some decent roads.'

'Oh, I'm not so sure,' I said. 'I am not so pleased with the modern street with its dreadful monotony, its long and high blank spaces and its dull pretentious uniformity repeated on either side of you down a mile long vista.'

'I have no desire for drabness,' smiled David, 'and I feel sorry for the humble citizen driven out, which has happened so often with the coming of the railways. The tracks have cut great swathes through our cities but increasing prosperity entails more and more vehicles on the roads. And suppose the genius of our inventors comes along with a train that runs without rails, a kind of horseless carriage for personal use? Where will we be then?'

'Now you are being fanciful,' laughed Harold. 'A horseless carriage indeed!'

In fact the traffic cleared somewhat as we fought our way through Piccadilly and in no time at all we were at the gates of the Jim-Jam Club.

'You stay here?' I said to David in some surprise.

'Oh, yes, my club in Brussels has a reciprocal arrangement with the Jim-Jam. Why, have you ever been here?'

'It's all right, David,' Harold broke in, 'I took Jenny to a Victor Pudendum contest not so long ago.'

'My,' said Doctor David Lezaine as Dodds came out from the club to open our carriage door and I could see that his merry dark eyes were twinkling at me in a new light.

Anyways, we refreshed the pickpocket, whose name was Austen Nicholas, with a slap-up meal and when David had unpacked and refreshed himself from his tiring journey, we all three sat quietly in one of the richly furnished lounges and listened to Austen's melancholy tale. We told him to speak candidly and to withdraw nothing for the sake of so-called rectitude. We wanted the truth, the whole truth and nothing but the truth.

As we sipped out brandies (there was no nonsense at the Jim-Jam about allowing only men the privilege of this excellent spirit after a meal), we listened intently to Austen who began:

'I am a clerk by profession and earned a good, round sum every week at Perkupp and Rubenstein's counting house in the City. As a single man, I was able to save a proportion of my wages and lived quite comfortably in my rooms in the Holloway Road, Islingtion.

'Then disaster struck me when Brenda, the pretty daughter of Mr Perkupp my principal, came into the office three months ago to see her Papa. She was a lovely girl some eight years younger than I, and I must confess that I was immediately enamoured of her beauty. She was, or is I should say, a most attractive woman with long black hair, a pair of large blue eyes and a pretty retrousse nose.

'"Good morning, Mister Nicholas," she said brightly as she passed my desk. She never failed to greet me on the previous visits and I returned her greeting. Unfortunately, her father was out and about half an hour after she had left, old Vine, the chief clerk called me into his office.

'"It seems that Miss Brenda has returned home a day earlier than expected from her friends down in Bournemouth," said the chief clerk, "and she needs some money rather urgently. Unfortunately, Mister Perkupp is with Sir Bernard Reuben, one of our most important clients, and cannot be disturbed. However, I am withdrawing twenty pounds from the petty cash and would ask you to deliver it to Miss Brenda this evening. You know that the Perkupp family resides in Highgate which is not too far from your lodgings. You may leave work one hour earlier than usual and I have also taken out a guinea for you so that you may go there and back by hansom. I'm sure you do not mind taking on this duty?"

'Did I mind! I should say not and I thanked old Vine for asking me to undertake the errand. I left the office in a state of excitement and arrived at six o'clock sharp at the imposing door of the Perkupp's house in a street just before one reaches the brow of Highgate Hill.

'I dismissed the cabby as I wanted so much to speak to Brenda. I had no reason to believe that I would be welcomed in and could well have been curtly dismissed at the door, handing over the money – "Is that the envelope with the twenty pounds? Thank you, Mister Nicholas. Good evening". Yet I hoped against hope that as she had to sign a receipt I could at least enter the house. After all, there was just the slightest possibility that she might want it explained and then I would at least have the chance to talk. Good old Vine! It was just like him to insist on obtaining a receipt.

'I was a stride away from the door when it opened and it was Brenda herself who had opened it. "Hello, Mister Nicholas, have you brought the money? Come in, do." And she led me through into the drawing room and I gave her the envelope explaining that I had a receipt for her to sign.

'"Give it to me and I'll sign it now," she said brightly, "and meanwhile give me your hat and take off your coat. You must be tired after coming all the way up here after a full day's work at the boring old office."

'I needed no second invitation and she deposited my hat and coat back in the hall, calling out to me to make myself comfortable. When she returned she signed the receipt and gave it back to me saying: "I am all alone here as the servants were given the day off and will not be returning until tomorrow. Bell the butler is out until ten so I am here all by myself.

'"Do take a seat, Mister Nicholas," she said. "Perhaps you will let me pour you a glass of wine?"

'I eagerly accepted her invitation and soon we were chatting away like old friends. I tried my best to be bright and entertaining though I was shy and worried about outstaying my welcome.

'Brenda had made up a selection of small sandwiches and put them out with some biscuits and before you could say Jack Robinson, we had finished a whole bottle of wine between us. Brenda insisted on my opening a second bottle of Cortonne '64 and we had consumed at least half of this when Brenda looked up at me, smiling sweetly, and said: "Do you know, we must have met at least half a dozen times Mister Nicholas but I still don't know your first name."

'"It's Austen," I replied, "and I know yours. It's Brenda, is it not?"

'"Yes, well that's all right, then. Now we have been properly introduced!" she laughed. "Look, are you doing anything tonight? Would you like to stay and have some supper? I see that Mrs Bridges has left some nice slices of cold meat and we can easily make up a salad. We can finish off our simple meal with some fruit salad. I hope you do not think me forward but I do not enjoy being here alone though I would of course enjoy your company for its own sake. Bell should be back by ten though I will wager he will be late as I have a strong suspicion that he is fucking the cook at our friends' round the corner in Cholmondley Gardens. However, that is his affair."

'I must have shown my shock at her freeness with words as she giggled delightfully, saying: "Oh, Austen, I see I have surprised you by my rather free speech. I'm afraid that was the wine speaking just now!"

'"Well you know what they say, Brenda," I replied boldly, "in *vino veritas*!"

'"In wine there is truth," she translated, still giggling, "but of course a young City clerk like you living all alone cannot know too much about fucking."

'"I cannot claim as much experience as I would like," I retorted, draining my glass. "But I have had my moments even if the last fuck I enjoyed was several months ago."

'"And since then you have had to resort to tossing off?" she said looking at me straight in the eye.

'I really was taken aback by her brazenness but my heart began to beat at a rate of knots when she stood up, moved her hands up her thighs under her dress and to my delighted amazement pulled down her drawers.

'I felt the swell of a hard-on as with an almost mad abandon she kicked off her shoes and began to undress. In no time at all she stood naked in front of me, obviously enjoying the way I was goggling at her. Her long, tousled hair shimmered in the evening light. She stretched and arched her back, then caressing her own heavy breasts she walked towards me.

'She stood just inches before me and her pubic moss was staring me full in the face. I kissed her belly and then ran my tongue lower, through the strands of her silky bush. My hands circled around her glorious bum cheeks as I buried my head between her thighs and drew her against me. My tongue now crept down into her slit which was already nice and wet. She gasped and shivered as I found her clitoris and began to roll my tongue around the erectile piece of flesh.

'"Oh!, Oh! Aaaaaah!" she moaned. "You are a marvellous sucker! Mmmmmmm, that's gorgeous. Oh Austen, quickly now, take off your clothes and put your cock inside me!"

'Who could resist such a command? I threw off my clothes and soon we were locked together in a naked embrace, my stiff cock throbbing up against her tummy as our mouths meshed together in a burning kiss, our tongues splashing around in each other's mouths.

'Brenda continued to make the running, so to speak, as she pushed me back in an easy chair and murmured: "I'm going to sit on your lovely thick cock, Austen, and you will feel it gliding juicily into my moist little cunt." And she was as good as her word, striding my legs but leaving her pussey just next to as opposed to on top of my straining cock. She took my hands and placed them on her stiff little titties. I moved over them with my palms which seemed to excite her even more. Now she moved up and over my cock which she took in her hand and guided it firmly into her lubricated love-channel. She sat down on it, trapping the entire length of it in her engorged cunt. She wriggled with pleasure as she bounced up and down, leaning forward to let her heavy breasts dangle in front of my face. I was mere putty in her hands as I felt my raging prick impale her willing cunney and automatically my hips pushed up to meet her downward thrusts.

'She increased the speed and my cock seeemed to swell up

even bigger than before. My cock twitched and jerked and I gushed out jets of semen as I spent copiously inside her and we both whimpered with joy at every spasm as she spent too so that our love juices mingled together in a veritable flood of mutual jism.

'My cock still retained much of its stiffness and Brenda motioned me to follow her as we went out of the room and sped upstairs into her bedroom. We flung ourselves down and began kissing and cuddling again. We lay in a sort of sixty-nine position with Brenda's thighs clasped round my head and her spunk coated pussey lips pressed firmly against my mouth. As I licked up the morsels of our previous repast, she sucked my cock up to full erection and then, to my great delight, licked around that sensitive area between my arsehole and my balls. A tongue run down there drives me insane. After giving that area a good going over, Brenda transferred her wicked little tongue to the head of my cock, flicking at it with the very tip of her tongue so expertly that I could feel my balls tightening and my prick now rocklike hard.

'We disengaged and she lay on her back, her legs open and her pink pussey lips jutting through the blackness of her hairy mound. I sank my rigid tool into the warm softness and I felt the walls of her cunt clamp round my cock which was madly pumping in and out of her, sliding deep, deep, grinding my trusty prick against her clitty. I felt her climax to be near so I pressed my finger against her clitty, holding my cock still inside her as spasm after spasm shook her lovely body. "Carry on fucking, Austen," she gasped, "I want more of that spunky juice inside me."

'She began to come, shivering and trembling as she reached the apex and I felt her cunney grip my cock even harder as she entered the throes of orgasm. With her hands gripping my bum I found myself thrusting in and out of her cunney at an even speedier rate and soon the spunk was boiling up in my balls and I exploded into her, filling her pussey with gushes of frothy sperm. We screamed loudly in the frenzy of emission and Brenda almost fainted away with delight as I slumped exhausted upon her senseless body.

'We then rested and I lay my head down on her beautiful big titties while she gently played with my limp cock.'

Here Austen drew breath and after listening so intently to this stirring tale, so graphically recounted, I too slumped back feeling as though I had been well fucked myself!

'I fail to see why all this should be so upsetting for you,' said Harold Le Meshigunah. 'It seems to me as though you found yourself in clover – is that the right expression, Jenny?'

'That's right, Harold,' I said, 'and to be honest, I cannot see what is causing you such great distress. Wait a minute, though, did the silly girl neglect to take any precautions against getting into the Club?'

Austen shook his head and sighed: 'No, that wasn't the problem. To continue to the end of the tale, we fucked again a little later and then we washed and dressed so to be composed when Bell returned which he did only ten minutes past ten so it was as well that we assumed punctuality on his behalf. From the smile on his plump face, we also assumed that he had managed to bed the cook from Cholmondley Gardens and I bid Brenda good night feeling "on top of world" as the saying goes.

'I strolled down Highgate Hill, enjoying the walk as it was a fine night, when I heard footsteps behind me.'

'Footpads,' I breathed. 'I was reading in *The Times* only the other day how many robberies are being committed on the highway by snatching with violence from the unwary traveller.'

'Yes, Jenny, it was a pair of footpads and as one of them passed me by he made a snatch at my silver chain, breaking it with a violent wrench. As I gave chase, the second ruffian wrestled with me so that I would not catch his comrade. But as luck would have it, I quickly tripped him and he fell over, twisting his ankle which left him unable to follow me as I chased the robber down the hill. Good fortune stayed with me for as the thief approached the Archway, he too tripped over a piece of wood and went sprawling into the gutter. I caught him up, and dragged him to his feet. I pulled what I thought was my watch out of his pocket and roughly pushed him away. "You scoundrel," I exclaimed. "I have half a mind to call a constable!" But despite the shock of the attempted robbery, I was in a good mood, thinking of that glorious fuck I had enjoyed earlier in the evening, so with a stern remonstrance, I let him slink back up the hill to rejoin his friend, who was hobbling slowly towards us.

'I managed to catch an omnibus to my lodgings and when I took out my watch to see if it had been damaged in the commotion, I discovered that not only had I reclaimed my watch from the villain but also a small packet of sovereigns, no doubt the proceeds of an earlier felony.

'There were thirteen gold coins in the packet and I had no way of returning them. I suppose I could have gone to a police station but frankly, who knows when the robbery or robberies that had yielded this haul had taken place. Indeed, some of the money could have actually belonged to the man. But in the end I decided to read the evening papers carefully and if any robbery in the locality had been reported which could have been carried out by my assailants, I would then mention what had happened to me to the police.'

'This gets better and better!' I laughed. 'First you partake of a delicious fuck and then you find that you have been well-paid for it!'

'Alas, Miss Everleigh,' said Austen sadly, 'I am afraid that there is a sting in the tail.'

I could not help smiling at his unintentional pun but Harold and David told him not to mind my unwanted interruption and to conclude his story.

He continued: 'I went to work the next day in the best of spirits but in the evening, as I was composing a letter of thanks to Brenda and hoping that I would have the pleasure of seeing her again, I was bothered by an itching sensation in my groin. I thought little of it and washed myself thoroughly before retiring and settled down to a good night's sleep.

'But I was kept awake all night by an increasing discomfort all round the base of my prick and in the morning, to my horror, I saw that I had been infected with an infestation of tiny crab-like creatures scuttling around my pubic hair. It was a most alarming experience! I rushed into a pharmacy and was given some ointment which the druggist assured me would kill these devilish little lice and as it happens the preparation worked wonderfully and I was completely cured in a few days.'

'Yes, the infestation is not totally uncommon,' smiled David Lezaine. 'But you should avoid contact with others until the "crabs", as they are commonly known, clear up and give in your undergarments to the laundry as soon as you have taken them off.'

'Yes, Yes,' said Austen, 'I was told all this by the druggist. My problem was that it was obviously Brenda who had infected me. What was I to say to her?

'As it happened, I had no cause to worry about this matter because just two days later, my employer, Mister Perkupp, called me into his office and, with only a brief word, gave me notice of instant dismissal. There had been no complaint about the quality of my work so I knew that my encounter with Brenda must have been the cause. What on earth had Brenda told her father? As I left the office, in somewhat of a daze as you can well imagine, I saw Brenda alighting from a hansom. I rushed over to her and begged her to speak to her father on my behalf.

'"Why should I intercede for you," she hissed. "You gave me crabs, you horrible man. I told Papa that you had insulted me when you came round to the house and behaved too freely. That is why you were sacked today."

'"I did not give you crabs," I said indignantly. "You gave them to me. I hadn't been intimate for at least three months before I met you so you must have caught them from someone else."

'"I don't believe you," she said. "The only other man who could possibly have infected me has told me he is absolutely clean and I have no reason to disbelieve him. After all, he is a curate!"'

'Oh dear,' said Harold gloomily, 'I don't believe in our reverendo's denial for a moment. So often these pulpit moralisers about the so-called sins of the flesh are hypocritical.'

'I don't know about that,' shrugged Austen, 'but the sad conclusion of the matter is that for the last four months I have been out of work and frankly my chances of securing employment grow more remote every day. I was given no letter of reference and without references, it is impossible to find a job.

'I have pawned almost everything I own and if it had not been for the fourteen sovereigns I accidentally stole from the footpad, I would now be starved to death or find myself in a workhouse, a fate worse than death! I must pay my landlady her back rent tomorrow or I will be thrown out onto the street and as I am an orphan and totally without family, I just did not know which way to turn! So I set off for a railway terminus for I remember reading in a newspaper as to how many pickpockets were operating at the main railway stations and I am ashamed to say that is how you came to make my acquaintance this morning. I am normally extremely nimble with my hands but hunger had weakened my abilities.

'I count myself blessed by Dame Fortune that such noble, charitable folk as your good selves have offered me succour,' he concluded.

We were profoundly touched by Austen Nicholas's sad story but I am glad to relate that, as in the best of tales, this one does have a happy ending. Harold knew that his accountant was in need of a senior clerk and upon his recommendation, Austen secured a post there and I sincerely hope that he prospers there.

November 8th, 1871

To the theatre last night, dear diary, along with my old friend Louisa Goring and Johnny who nobly escorted us both to The Lyceum where Mr Mansfield had revived *King Richard III*. It was a fine performance, well staged and well acted. Mr Mansfield gave us a whole-hearted portrait of the crook-backed tyrant – not ringletted as we can remember him from our schooldays, but with a more martial bearing added to a more bloodthirsty and fiendish temper. There is a horrible snarl with which he reaks away from his hypocritical ways and his hand is always seeking his sword or dagger.

The most competent authorities have watched over its production and the way it has been staged at the Globe is wonderful. The fighting is intensely real and Richard hacks about him with the light of battle in his eyes and the strength of battle in his arm. In earlier scenes he was subdued but the malignant demon came out as the play advanced. I thrilled at Mr Mansfield's performance when, throwing off the mask of hypocrisy and throwing his breviary into the air with it, he stood confessed the fiendish tyrant. His make-up was capital, his costumes magnificent and the whole performance was a thoughtful, highly original one.

Even the generally irrepressible tattlers in the private boxes, and those folk who feel compelled to make running commentaries upon the scene on the stage in front of them, were subdued into silence. The slightest noise in the gallery was immediately checked and if the stalls had dared to chatter, I truly believe that the pit would have had their blood.

Anyhow, we dined at Nolan's Chop House in St James's

before Johnny hailed a hansom and gave the driver an order to proceed to Albion Square.

'Johnny, should we not take Louisa home first?' I said.

'No, Lord and Lady Goring are at a house-party out of town,' said Johnny with a strange gleam in his eye.

'I hope you don't mind my coming with you,' said Louisa, a veritable beauty of no more than nineteen, blessed with a slender figure, an elegant aristocratic countenance and a white, unblemished skin.

We made ourselves comfortable in the lounge whilst Johnny opened a bottle of champagne that he had instructed his servant to keep in a bucket of ice. She was now upstairs in the garret asleep, so we could enjoy our total privacy.

We were all feeling somewhat randy and I needed little encouragement to feel Johnny's cock which was tenting through his trousers when he suddenly grabbed hold of my breasts and began rolling them around in his hands.

'Johnny, stop it,' I murmured somewhat half-heartedly, 'what will Louisa think of us?'

'Louisa thinks she would like to join!' said the gorgeous girl, unbuttoning her blouse, and before long we were all naked and enjoying a threeway kiss, pressing our lips together and a *ménage à trois* was about to begin.

Johnny whispered to me: 'I have a fancy to see you suck Louisa's pussey, it would give me great joy.' He disengaged himself and stood magnificently naked, his thighs spread and his superb prick standing straight out from the thicket of pubic hair. However, I was almost as excited by the delicious body of Louisa who stretched herself out on the floor, her hands jiggling her firm, uptilted breasts in a most inviting fashion.

I lay down beside her and leaning over, kissed her upright little nipples, twirling my tongue around them. I flicked them up to a fine state of erection and then let my mouth travel slowly along her soft skin downwards to her crotch.

I caressed her wonderful buttocks with my hands as my own nipples, hard with desire, tracked down the length of her. My lips were now only inches away from her down-covered pussey. Instinctively she opened her legs to make the wet, swollen lips more accessible and I paused for a moment to savour the musky aroma and I kissed the pink pussey lips which were aching to be opened by my questing tongue.

Lovingly, I began to eat her, forcing my tongue deep into the juicy pit, sliding up and down her crack and I heard her gasp with pleasure as I probed between her cunney lips and found her clitty. I rolled it between my lips, sucking furiously as she shouted in delight, throwing her body all over the place and I had a hard time staying with her as she rubbed herself off against my mouth.

Johnny was watching this action intently and he was so taken by it that he began to play with his swollen cock. I had no desire for Johnny to waste his spend so I pulled my lips away from Louisa's dripping pussey for a moment and told Johnny 'to go behind!'

He needed no second urging and knelt behind me as I raised my backside in the air, opening my legs slightly so he could guide the tip of his cock into my wet cunt. I raised and wriggled my bum but, alas, too late and all he succeeded in doing was coming all over my arse at the same time that Louisa was pouring out her libation all over my tongue.

They had both spent but I felt left out though Johnny came to my rescue by burying his face in my pussey and lapped at my cunney, driving me to the ultimate pleasure.

'My turn,' I murmured and I turned on my back on the thick pile carpet, stroking my thighs sensuously. The fire-light was playing across my body, highlighting the golden hairs of my bush but it was Louisa whose hand slid between my legs and rose into the cleft of my cunney. I grabbed her hair and pushed her sweet face into my crotch and she nuzzled against my cunney lips, kissing and sucking in great delight. She kissed the inside of my thighs as my legs opened wider and her naughty hand slipped into me. Oh, how her fingers twisted and turned inside my cunt and it was as though an electric current had been passed through me and I could feel the moisture fairly dripping down the inside of my thighs.

Then Louisa pushed her head back between my legs and sucked noisily on my cunney, her lips sliding into my womb sending shivers of pleasure speeding through me. Johnny knelt down by me, holding his stiff and glistening cock that jutted out so delightfully from the hairy moss at the base of his flat belly. I took hold of the throbbing tool as he leaned across me and bestrode me in a quick movement so that his legs were either side of me. I was now in a better position to kiss and suck his lovely cock which I did with great relish, capping and uncapping the darling purple helmet. I sucked up his prick to its fullest erection and my other hand reached behind him, probing for the cleft of his buttocks, setting up a rhythmic motion and I cupped his balls and felt a tightening which occurs when the sperm begins its journey upwards to the head of the penis.

I did not want Johnny to waste his cum as before so I immediately ceased my ministrations and said: 'Please Johnny, change places with Louisa as I do so want you to fuck me.'

Nothing loath, Louisa jumped up and suckled my titties with her hand and mouth whilst I pulled Johnny on top of me, guiding his prick with my hands so that he entered easily especially as my juices were flowing down because of Louisa's expert munching of my motte. Johnny mounted me, the tip of his cock inside me.

'More, more,' I cried. 'Ram your cock right inside my cunt!' I raised my hips sharply to meet him, forcing more of the shaft deeper and it slid out as I fell back. On stiffened arms he kept his cock from full entry but then with an almighty groan he drove down and I took in the whole of his cock from tip to root as our pubic hairs enjoined. I wrapped my legs around his waist as Louisa slid a cushion under my hips to intensify the pressure of his cock against my pubes. As his strokes became more insistent I spent again and again and again as Johnny now went rigid and caught his breath. I felt his semen squirt into me and as his cock twitched preparatory to spurting, I squeezed on the shaft tightly, releasing a lovely, sensuous orgasm that burst deep within me.

This set Louisa off again for she insisted on squeezing Johnny's balls and sucking his cock until he managed a third fine erection. She then got astride his hips where with a single downwards motion she impaled herself on his gorgeous tool. With long, lingering strokes she slid her hungry pussey up and down the towering length of Johnny's cock as we girls kissed and cuddled and Johnny's hands were busy fingering our cunnies which kept his excitement at fever pitch. Louisa's cunney began to dry up somewhat so I took a turn at planting Johnny's prick between my legs and I crooned with glee as it entered my sopping nest. Oh, the joy of a hot stiff cock in one's cunt! Is there anything more pleasurable in the world than a powerful, considerate lover with a thick, upstanding prick?

As Louisa's cunney had now recovered, I entreated her to climb back on the love pole, an invitation which she eagerly accepted, and she thanked me for my kindness.

'It is but a small favour, darling Louisa,' I said. 'After all, I can have Johnny's cock up me most nights but for you it is a new and rare experience.'

As the hours passed we fucked in a variety of postures until Johnny pleaded for an end to the proceedings. 'There is no doubt that we are by far the stronger sex,' teased Louisa. 'I am sure that we could continue for much longer but just look at this cock!' And she flipped up Johnny's limp shaft in a gesture of derision.

'Good grief, what you need is a stable of studs!' cried Johnny. 'Few men can fuck as many times on the trot as I have done tonight.

'You girls are surely not complaining,' he added hoarsely.

'No, no, my sweet, I think your cock deserves ten out of

ten for his efforts. It is just that we girls are still feeling frisky.'

'You will have to play with yourselves,' groaned Johnny and with a great sigh he turned on his side and in an instant was fast asleep.

November 16th, 1871

Me tamen urit amor; quis enim adsit amori. Virgil.
Love consumes me yet – for what bound may be set to love?

The English Horse Show Society Exhibition at Olympia attracted a large crowd and Johnny and I met up with some friends to see the riding and the jumping. We sat near the Royal Box and I am sure that the Prince of Wales returned my little wave of the hand as he sat down after formally declaring the Show open.

We were part of Colonel Clarke's party which included young Lord Montairy and his cousin, the well-known Society beauty, The Honourable Cecilia Jerome, as well as Lieutenant Dickson Berry and his fiancée Diana FitzNicely, and Major Rodney O'Toole who partnered a pretty young lady whose name I did not fully catch when we were introduced. Her first name was Lizzie but though her face was familiar to me, I just could not place where I had seen it before.

I best enjoyed the jumping for the fences were of such a nature that those of us in the reserved seats could see nearly every kind of fence to be found in Britain negotiated in its own peculiar style. For instance, in addition to the double, single, gate and water jump, there was the stone wall of Gloucestershire, Scotland and Galway.

I must record the admirable driving in the four-in-hand won by Lord Rothschild's excellent coachman, Simmons, and indeed the sensation of the show, the jumping of Mr Taylor's Sugar Plum who, with a long coat on and ridden in rusty bit and irons created no end of laughter when she came in; but equal applause when she took the bank and double at a mouthful, never touching the bank even with a hind shoe.

Colonel Clarke had kindly invited the party to dine at his impressively large house facing the Thames in Cheyne Walk. It was detached and stood back in its own grounds. We were ushered in by two handsome young Indian footmen who escorted our party into the dining room where a sumptuous buffet was laid out.

'Help yourselves,' cried out the hospitable colonel. 'As we missed tea, I am sure you must all be ravished.'

'Hell, if we are not ravished now it's odds-on we will be later,' grinned Cecilia Jerome. I was shocked at this levity but as the rest of the company laughed heartily at the jest, I said nothing to Johnny who was stuffing his face with cold chicken salad washed down by a quite superb champagne.

Colonel Clarke invited us to sit at the two tables laid out in the spacious room and I realized that we were nicely proportioned between the sexes. Besides Johnny and myself there were three other couples with our host the odd man out which I thought rather a shame and I said so quietly to Johnny who to my surprise gave a big grin and said: 'Dear me, Jenny, you must know full well why Dennis Clarke is on his own this evening.'

'I do not, Johnny, otherwise why should I have mentioned the fact to you?' I replied, a little cross at the way he trifled with my request.

'You really do not know?'

'Johnny, if I knew I would not be asking you,' I said with as much patience as I could muster.

He could see that I was getting angry and his jaw dropped. 'Jenny, my darling, do forgive me. I keep forgetting that you are new to London Society ways and that Colonel Clarke's little soirées are hardly likely to be reported in the Press. Mind, there was talk last summer that an art critic did discover H R H one evening at Cheyne Walk but I understand that Sir Louis Segal managed to hush up the matter by giving the fellow a well-paid job in his New York gallery.'

Oh, ho, I thought, what does this evening hold in store? My question was soon answered when the footmen cleared away the remains of our extremely palatable buffet feast and Colonel Clarke sat down at the piano.

'Well, my friends, I think the time has come to hold our own Chelsea Horse Show. All in favour, please signify in the usual way.'

All the other guests had been at one of the Colonel's parties before as they chorused their assent by taking off their shoes. 'Go on, Jenny take off your shoes,' urged Johnny, so not to appear rude I followed suit.

Colonel Clarke sat down on the piano stool. I thought he played quite marvellously but Lord Montairy, who with Cecilia Jerome was sitting at our table, whispered somewhat unkindly: 'I say, old Dennis does try hard, he really does but I fear that he will never improve to concert hall standards no matter how hard he tries.'

He played two waltzes that were familiar to me and then attempted a Chopin polonaise. He played with dash and style and the performance possessed strength and exuberance yet even I, with my limited knowledge of music, felt that he missed the nervous melancholy, the wistful gaiety and slightly faded romance of Chopin's work.

We applauded politely and two further magnums of champagne were distributed around the company. Colonel Clarke tossed off half a tumbler and turning back to the piano he played the opening bars of a familiar old chorus.

'I can't recall the name of that song,' drawled Cecilia to Lord Montairy. 'Would you kindly remind me of its name, dearest Cecil.'

'It is *The Hound That Caught The Pubic Hair*, my sweet,' said his noble lordship and we all gave a great laugh at his quick jest.

'I heard that,' called out the colonel. 'Let's open the proceedings with a game of Rollicking Rhyming. You all know how to play, I take it? Oh, Miss Everleigh you don't know the rules, do you? Well, I shall play the first verse or so of a song and then we go through the company with each member having to supply an instant lyric for the next line. Only ten seconds are allowed for thought.

'If the company votes the line a winner, the contestant nominates another member of the group who has to divest him or herself of an article of clothing. If the line is voted a loser, the rhymer has to take off an article of his or her own clothing. It is a good game, I warrant you, and I am sure you will enjoy it.

'We'll start with you, Rodney, and work clockwise round your table and then go on to Cecil Montairy and work clockwise round his group. Are you all ready? Here we go!'

He struck up a chorus and began:

'At the Horse Show, such a beezer
Rodney felt Lizzie's tits oh they were such a teaser,
Though they had a plaid rug to cover their front –'

'Er, er,' stammered Rodney as we began to chant: 'One, two, three, four' and then his quick Irish wit produced:

'My prick stood up as I felt Lizzie's cunt.'

By acclaim, Rodney's rhyme was adjudged successful and he nominated his fair companion to divest heself of her stockings. She did so to the polite applause of the gathering and now it was Lizzie's turn as the Colonel sang:

'We watched the jumping, such fine sport,
I never refused when he passed the port,
At the first fence a filly fell –'

'And so did I at a posh hotel!' finished Lizzie with a flourish.

'Bravo! Bravo!' we cried and Lieutenant Berry called out: 'Fizzbuzz! Fizzbuzz!'

'What on earth is "Fizzbuzz",' I asked Johnny.

'Ah, that means that we must vote as to whether the rhyme is worthy of high distinction. If we vote "yes" then the person designated by the rhymer must divest himself of two pieces of attire. If we vote against, however, the "Fizzbuzz" proposer must take off two articles of clothing! So be careful only to shout out "Fizzbuzz" if you think the rhyme is of the best quality.'

By general consent the company voted with Lieutenant Berry and Lizzie was given her choice of victim. 'As you made me take off my stockings, I propose that you take off your socks and your trousers, Rodney!' she giggled and we gave a rousing 'Hear, Hear' at our table.

Rodney's socks were off in a trice but he made great play about pulling down his trousers.

'Let me help you,' offered Lizzie.

'Oh I say, thanks awfully,' said Rodney. 'These trousers are so damned tight that it might take more than even two pairs of hands to get them off.'

'I'll help too,' shrieked Diana FitzNicely, and with a flourish began opening Rodney's fly buttons.

The girls eased off Rodney's bags without too much trouble and Lizzie could not resist plunging her hand into the gap in his undershorts and brought out his long pink cock to be admired by all the guests. She gave it a quick little rub but then withdrew her hand for she did not wish her man to be overstimulated before the fucking began in earnest.

'That's a fine looking prick, young man,' said Colonel Clarke. 'I hope you will know where to put it a little later in the proceedings. Time now for the next verse. Let me see now, looking at that table, how about –

'So Lizzie played with his balls and thought it no harm,
He fingered her quim and ne'er felt alarm,
His cock was formed for a maiden to please –

'And his bollocks hung down very near to his knees!' finished Dickson Kerry with a flourish, winning another 'Fizzbuzz' from us.

I will not bore you, dear diary, with the rest of the verses for in truth, we partook of so much wine that I can hardly remember them.

What I do remember though was after two or three rounds of this jolly game, the whole company, except for Colonel Clarke, was stark naked and the men's cocks were all up in a fine state of erection.

We ranged up in a semi-circle after the men had carefully pulled a couch into the middle of the room. We needed no further orders from Colonel Clarke who sat at the piano, his flies open, his prick jutting upwards as he viewed the orgiastic affair that was unfolding in his room.

'Now, Jenny, as you are as yet uninitiated as far as Cheyne Walk parties go,' said the gallant Lord Montairy, 'I think it only right and proper that you begin proceedings by kissing our cocks.'

I blushed but acceded to his command and took Johnny's thick prick in my right hand and Rodney's longer yet thinner prick in the other. I gave them both a good rub to bring them up to full height so they stood up against their bellies like two little flagpoles. Then, getting down on my knees, I pulled them gently together and took both the gleaming red heads into my mouth, washing them both over with my tongue, causing them to moan loudly with ecstacy. 'Now, Dickson, you may enter Jenny from behind,' said my noble lord, so I raised my bottom as I leaned forward, still with the two pricks in my mouth, and the young soldier positioned the uncapped head of his rubicund charger between my bottom cheeks but alas, he was unable to restrain his excitability and he spent almost immediately over my bum, the sperm coming out in frothy white spurts as he rubbed the shaft to extract the last drains of his spendings.

Diana FitzNicely kindly wiped as much of the sperm off

my bum as she could and inserting her slim fingers into my crack from behind, she lubricated my pussey with Dickson's spend.

I continued to lick and lap at the two pricks that filled my mouth as I heard Lord Montairy say: 'Bad luck, old fellow! Never mind, it could happen to anyone. Let me have a go.'

Cecilia, as was right and proper as she was Lord M's *amour*, took hold of his noble cock and directed it properly to my cunt dripping with the manual lubrication provided by Diana. His cock entered my cunney with a lovely squelch and I pushed out my bum to receive as much of this ramrod stiff shaft as possible.

The two pricks were bounding and swelling in my mouth as I jerked my hands up and down the swollen shafts. Together they spurted creamy globs of spunk into my mouth and I took every last drop until both pricks shrunk down to half mast.

Lord Mountairy was still happily pushing his prick in and out of my cunt from behind and my entire body quivered as he rammed home, sheathing his cock so fully that his balls banged against my bum cheeks.

'Oh, what joy! What bliss!' he cried out as he leaned forward to fondle my lush breasts and erect little titties. I waggled my arse provocatively and this artful manoeuvering led to my aristocratic young man sending spout after spout of spunk into my juicy cunney and later Johnny told me that he could almost see the ripples of orgasmic joy running down my spine as we shuddered to a flawless mutual climax.

'My goodness, what happiness,' I gasped, 'or perhaps I should say that as would a French lady, my goodness, what a penis!'

My witticism was greeted by a gale of laughter and we all partook of a refreshing glass of champagne.

Rodney's blood was up and he grabbed hold of Diana FitzNicely and kissed her large nipples with great passion until they stood up like twin rosebuds; I admired her white belly that was so well set off at the bottom by a glossy black pubic mound. She possessed a quite splendid mount and whilst Rodney continued to squeeze her ample breasts, Lizzie, on her hands and knees, scrambled between them to slip one hand round Rodney's thickening cock and the other into the black hair that surrounded Diana's pussey. She soon parted the serrated cunt-lips with her tapering fingers and began rubbing and pinching the projecting clitty with her thumb and forefinger.

'Rub it harder, harder please, you sweet girl, Ooooh! Oooh!' cried Diana as she imprisoned the hand between her legs, wrapping it tightly between her jerking thighs as she built up to a climax.

Lizzie's left hand was busy frigging Rodney's long cock, which she teased up to a fine state of erection by kissing the purple uncapped dome, licking her way round the sensitive rim. Now she opened her mouth wide, enclosing her lips around it as tightly as she could, working the loose skin up and down the shaft whilst sucking on the dome with gusto and taking in as much of the long shaft as she was able into her mouth.

My clever Johnny grabbed two cushions and lay them behind Lizzie so she could play with Diana's sopping cunney and suck Rodney's prick in comfort. Johnny's cock was now standing stiffly to attention as he sank to his knees and parted Lizzie's legs to give us all a sight of the silky blonde mane that prettily covered the base of her belly. Lizzie took her hand away from Rodney's cock, which was being munched in her mouth to their mutual joy, to slip Johnny's rock-hard prick into her quim and she worked her hips up and down, letting his throbbing cock sink all the way into her juicy snatch.

It was now Colonel Clarke's turn to enter the fray and to my surprise made not for Cecilia or myself but promptly took up a position behind Rodney, and wetting his rather small prick with spittle, drove it up between Rodney's bum-cheeks into his bum-hole. As it was so small an instrument,

Rodney did not feel it too much as he only gave a little wriggle and took a hand away from Diana's titties to grasp the Colonel's balls that were banging against his buttocks and gave them a gentle squeeze.

However, the Colonel's deviancy gave Dickson the chance to attempt a second fuck with me which he did most delightfully, first laying me down and making my cunney moist with anticipation as he placed his head between my legs and ran his tongue very lightly along the edge of my slit. Oh, Dickson was even better than Johnny with his tongue, licking and lapping at such a speed that I felt that I was being properly fucked before his prick entered me! I lay back enjoying the blissful experience, when a second fine prick loomed over my head, belonging of course to Lord Montairy who just before had participated in one of the most enjoyable fucks in which it has ever been my pleasure to indulge. I wrapped my fingers round the base of the fleshy stiff shaft and as Dickson's fingers slotted in and out of my sopping pussey, I wanked his slick, velvety tool, slipping the skin of the shaft on and off the red mushroom head.

This was all quite delicious but I wanted to be fully satisfied so I said to Dickson: 'You tongue my cunney marvellously, Dickson, but I need your cock inside me.'

Straightaway, the dear lad got up and repositioned himself, lowering his manly torso gently on top of me, and his lovely prick slid into my hungry pussey. He began pumping up and down in a steady rhythm and I rose to meet his ardour as every pounding jab struck home. I managed to slow him down, making sure that on each stroke the whole of his superb cock slid in and out of me like a piston. His eyes were closed and he had a dreamy look on his pretty face as his hands fondled my breasts. I whimpered with joy at each thrust as I continued with my right hand to toss off Cecil Montairy's gorgeous tool. I felt his lordship's tool twitch madly in my hand and before I could take evasive action, a fountain of sperm jetted across my breasts.

Luckily, the cascade missed Dickson who was still fucking

me quite wonderfully and who added to the pleasure by licking up Lord Montairy's spunk from my titties.

'Oh, yes, oh, yes, Dickson, ah, those superb powerful strokes and – ah, make me spend, make me spend! Shoot your sperm!' I cried. 'Ram that cock inside me!'

We dissolved in a glorious frenzy of voluptuousness and I spent time and again as he jetted his boiling juice up my love-channel into my womb. I so far forgot myself as to bite his shoulder in delight until at last he withdrew his now shrunken penis, glistening with my wetness that had flowed out of me like a river that had burst its banks.

I was now feeling quite tired but Rodney (never was there a man more aptly surnamed O'Toole!) and Cecilia treated us all to a sweet exhibition fuck. Rodney was no mere Irish cockney but a scion of an old Kilkenny family and Cecilia's breeding showed in her lovely soft skin and patrician features.

Colonel Clarke placed a pillow under Cecilia's bum and Rodney planted himself on his knees, between her thighs. They sat still for a moment or two, enjoying the mutual sensation of expectant repletion and possession so delightful to each of the participators in a loving fuck before commencing their performance.

A more beautiful couple it would be hard to conceive; he was a fine, strapping fellow with fair hair and brown eyes whilst her brunette complexion was almost a counterpart of his; and the base of his prick too as well as her pussey was ornamented with curly black hair. As she reached out to draw back the foreskin, the fiery purple head of his cock looked like a large ruby as he presented it to the luscious slit, the lips of which were slightly open as she lay with her legs apart. He rubbed his fat cock up and down her slit until she pleaded with him to pop it inside her. He first sucked her titties as her hand found his ivory hard tool and began to toss him off.

His cock looked so hard that I judged it best that it began its journey to Elysium so I took hold of it and nudged the tip just a little bit between her cunney lips. When Rodney had pushed all of his prick inside her, Cecilia let out a sigh of pleasure as her pussey was engorged with his throbbing tool. He began to push in and out and as he withdrew his prick we could see the gleaming wetness of Cecilia's juices shining on the shaft. Now the motions began to increase in speed as the energetic young man's balls knocked against her bum-hole as she twisted and panted and then hugging his heaving buttocks, she inserted a finger between them and into his bottom-hole which caused Rodney to snort and prance and then with a tremendous groan, he spurted his seed inside her and my own cunney began to throb as I saw the sweet girl spend in torrents of that ecstacy.

What heavenly joy it is to spend together in that combat of bliss that nature has afforded us! We fucked and sucked for some hours. At one time Lord Montairy's cock was in Cecilia's cunt whilst Lizzie was playing with her bottom-hole with a dildo in one hand whilst in the other she was tossing off Colonel Clarke. Lizzie was being fucked by Rodney who was playing delightfully with my cunt as I was sucking Dickson's thick prick whilst Johnny was presenting the red-headed dome of his cock to my bum-hole whilst he darted his tongue in and out of Diana's cunt which she pressed up against his face.

It was a house-party that I shall remember with pleasure, dear diary, as it was my first experience of an orgy. I enjoyed myself but I prefer to fuck in private. Still, one must experience as much of life as is possible – as the popular song has it (though admittedly in another context), one should 'suck it and see!'

Certainly, later this week, I shall see what happens on our visit to the Alfred Robbelow Academy for the Sons of Gentlefolk, an institution in which my family has taken an interest since my Great Uncle Peter was head boy some fifty years before. I am told there are some pretty young boys boarding at the school. I am sure I can devise a splendid prize or two for the scholars!

November 17th, 1871

As I woke up this morning, diary, I remembered where I had seen Lizzie's face (and her cunt!) before last night! It was of course on the train coming up to London some three months before when I enjoyed a most lascivious train journey with Lizzie, Yvonne Mainwearing and dear Johnny. It was the first lewd entry in your pages, diary. How on earth could I forget such an important affair!

More of Lizzie, anon, but first I must record what a splendid change in the weather we have enjoyed over the previous two days. Last week we were subjected to a horrible, poisonous fog. London's great nuisance can be most unpleasant and the 'Good mornings' that we mouthed as we cannoned off our friends in Grosvenor Place or Hyde Park Corner had a hollow ring in their tone. The grimy fiend abode with us for almost a week and morning after morning we rose to breathe a foul atmosphere, drawing in dirt and discomfort at every pore.

But I flung open the bedroom window and read a temperature of fifty-five degrees at 8.30 a.m. – this is surely a phenomenal November. I took only a light breakfast and wished Aunt Portia a successful day as she was off to Kempton Park with Major Bedford and I hoped that her horses would not prove as fickle as those of the gallant escort whose knowledge of horseflesh was supposedly comprehensive yet he failed to pick one winning mount the day before.

Soon afterwards Johnny arrived to take me down to Robbelow Academy where I was to present the Everleigh Memorial Prize for Public Speaking to the winner of the annual School debate. It was an onerous task as I was one of the judges nominated to select the winning speaker along with such distinguished luminaries as Sir Gerard Nolan and the Reverend Bernard Shaw. Someone from my family had always been to Founders Day to help judge the debate and as my dear parents were far away in the New World and as I was conveniently living in London, I was deputed to be the Everleigh representative on the panel.

My ever faithful Johnny kindly agreed to escort me to Croydon where the school was situated and, punctual as ever, he was ready and waiting by ten o'clock.

'Johnny, are you feeling well?' I asked. 'I was concerned that the exertions at Colonel Clarke's party might have exhausted you and that you would not be feeling well enough to taking me down to Croydon.'

'I am feeling fine and dandy, Jenny,' replied my true love. 'I have a request to make of you, however. You remember Lizzie, the blonde girl who performed so nobly last night?'

'It is truly coincidental that you should mention her name,' I said, 'for I was thinking of her only this morning. Do you know, we met her on the train coming up to London last August and neither of us recognised her!'

'I did, actually,' said my beloved, 'only I did not want to cause you any embarrassment by reminding you of the incident. Lizzie well recalled the journey we made together but she too said nothing in case you might have been embarrassed by the fact that we all fucked each other that afternoon.'

'How kind, but there was no cause for such modesty. I just failed to recognise her in all the excitement last night.'

'That's good. You see, her cousin, Philip, is a scholar at Robbelows and she would be most grateful if we could take her with us this morning as she would like to hear him speak in the debate.'

'I have no objection at all, Johnny, so long as you promise me that you will not engage in sexual dalliance with her – at least not before we have enjoyed the bliss of a loving fuck. I am not jealous by nature but I do believe that I am entitled to the first opportunity of enjoying any pleasure derived from your trusty cock.'

'Well said, Jenny,' he grinned, 'I give you my word indeed that you shall have first call on the services of my prick today and every day for as long as you may wish it so!'

We kissed and I felt Johnny's cock rise against me as we embraced, but this was not the time nor the place so we drove to pick up Lizzie from her parents' house in Exhibition Road, South Kensington.

The pretty blonde girl looked quite stunning in a simple brown silky dress and a small bonnet trimmed with white riband of the fashionable shape exposing the whole front of her head. Immediately we entered the carriage I explained that I had simply not placed her face last night and that I hoped she did not think that I was trying in any way to slight her. I was glad when she replied that no offence had been taken and that she was sure we would always remain the best of friends.

'How did you like Madam Kooshay's Equestrian School?' I asked her for I remembered that she and Yvonne had planned to spend a week there.

'It was quite fun,' she replied in a somewhat careless tone. 'I enjoy riding but both Yvonne and I were troubled by one of the instructors, one Major Horace Bounderby who was quite a good-looking man but was suffering from the contagion of *le vice anglais*.'

'*Le vice anglais*? I queried with a puzzled frown.

Johnny explained the phrase to me – 'This refers to men who cannot make their cocks swell unless they are walloped with a cane.'

'Good heavens, you mean they have to be smacked before any fucking?'

'More than smacked, Jenny, more like given a jolly good thrashing!' said Lizzie. 'Shall I tell you about poor old Horace? Yes? Well, he suffered from this very problem which began perhaps when his nanny used to play with his little willie when he was a small boy to soothe him to sleep. He then was sent to an old-fashioned public school where all the boys were beaten regularly and, this is only my speculation, you understand, he came to associate the whacking on his bum with the rubbing of the chair material against his cock.

'He was a handsome boy and was abused somewhat when he fagged for the prefects. One of them regularly pulled his trousers down and walloped his naked bottom with a plimsol whilst tossing off his prick at the same time.

'This has led to an association between pleasure and pain that has somehow never left poor Horace's noddle as this anecdote will show. He always eyed me lasciviously when I appeared in my tight riding breeches and my cream singlet showed well the soft, full swell of my breasts. I must confess that I knew that I had the Major in thrall, and one day, when we were in my room (I had made the pretext of asking him upstairs so I could lend him a book to read that afternoon) I deliberately dropped a piece of paper on the floor.

'I knelt on all fours to pick it up and took the opportunity of presenting Horace with a marvellous view of my bum. The tight trousers moulded the contours of my bum cheeks and as I pushed out my bum, the central seam of the trousers was strained like a hawser between the cheeks of my arse and under my legs. The material was so tight (I was wearing nothing underneath) that he could see the seam part the lips of my cunney!

'I heard Horace groan with unslaked desire and I drew myself upright and with a smile, pulled the singlet over the top of my head, letting him view my nude breasts which I cupped in my hands, stroking up my nipples to little peaks of hardness.

'Unless the man was a complete pansy, surely he would now fuck me! We kissed passionately and I said: "Let us both take off our clothes, I do so love making love naked. It is by far the most enjoyable mode of fucking."

'He sighed, his body rigid, much like a soldier's on parade, but he unbuttoned his shirt and removed his trousers. I pulled down his white linen drawers to view a thick, well formed cock which hung flaccidly down from a mass of wiry black pubic hair.

'I could not understand why that fine prick was not jutting proudly upwards ready and waiting for the wet embraces of my tongue and cunt! I kissed the tip and drew back the foreskin to uncover the helmet but despite taking it into my mouth and licking it all over, it obstinately refused to swell up even when I removed the rest of my clothes and stood quite naked in front of his gloating eyes.

'"Why, Horace, I thought you fancied me?" I said with a genuine note of reproach in my voice.

'"I do, Lizzie, I do," he said in a strained tone. "The fault lies solely within my peculiar state of mind.

'"If you want to help me to a cockstand," he added, "take up your riding crop that is standing up against the wall. I have been a naughty boy and I deserve six of the best. Cane me, Lizzie, and you shall see my old prick rise up as stiff as any rod you have ever seen."

'This was all new to me but my curiosity was aroused so when he bent over, I took up the crop and with some reluctance brought it fairly smartly down across his dimpled arse.

'"Harder, Lizzie, harder," he called out, waggling his bum.

'So I caned him again, this time with greater force and he arched his naked rump towards me. "That's the spirit, me dear," he shrieked, so doing his bidding, I really brought the stick across his bum as hard and with as much force as I was able to muster.

'"Crack away, Lizzie! Ah-r-r-re! How splendid, how invigorating! Cut away, my girl"'

'Obediently, I struck a further number of well-aimed cuts which quickly raised a warm, rosy tint so that, I must confess, an awakening interest crept into my own loins, that lovely familiar warmth that radiates out from the pussey to the breasts and then all over the body.

'I laid down the rod of chastisement and felt round to caress the previously flaccid cock. What a difference that beating had made to it! It was now standing stiffly to attention, and Horace himself drew back his foreskin making its purple helmet swell and bound in my hand.

'What a magnificent cockstand Horace could muster once he was aroused! The once soft tube of flesh was now as hard as rock and I could hardly grasp the breadth of it with my hand, even though as you can see, I possess longer than average fingers.

'I prefer my lovers to lick my pussey first but Horace was urgent to insert his rampant prick so I simply lay down and opened my legs so that he could enter me. How expertly he fucked me, pushing his massive cock slowly inside my willing cunney lips so that I could feel the full length of his shaft inside my cunt. He pumped away delightfully with a stroke in, hold, slip out . . . stroke in, hold, slip out . . . he made love with such controlled passion that I soon spent, my love juice coating his cock as it relentlessly ploughed its way in and out of my pussey. Then we pushed towards each other in shorter, more frantic motions as our lips fastened together as his hot spunk shot out into my innards, a streaming molten flood that washed the walls of my cunney and my whole womb felt as if it were swirling and shuddering around him.

'Our mouths came together now in a more leisurely kiss as we rested our warm bodies tenderly together, sinking into the bliss that follows the opening of the gates of love's reservoir.'

This lively tale was hugely welcome as it passed much of the time taken before we reached Robbelow's Academy. We made for the residence of the headmaster, Doctor Doolittle – known since his first day in office as Doctor Do-Bugger-All by the boys in his care and I dare say the good Doctor knew this but reflected that there was little he could do except bear the yoke cheerfully.

His house was situated near the village green, most conveniently placed just a quarter of a mile from the school itself which was purpose built for its work. It was a staid old house, where hoops and powder and patches, embroidered coats, rolled stockings, ruffles and swords had surely had their hours.

But Doctor Doolittle was a progressive headmaster and was keen to offer his boys the broadest possible education. As we sipped a refreshing glass of lemonade, for the Doctor was a strict teetotaller, he expounded his theory of education to us and to the other debating judges, Reverend Shaw and Sir Gerard Nolan, who had arrived together just minutes before us.

'Yes, my dear friends,' said the headmaster, 'I know that the utilitarian desire these days is for everyone to leave school trained to perform some task in life with expert skill. Yet this competence, however great, cannot pass for education in the fullest meaning of the word. For education is not merely learning, though I would never discourage the pursuit of knowledge for its own sake which has an important role to play.

'One meets people who are veritable mines of information, however, veritable walking encyclopaedias who cannot be described as being educated in the wider, worthwhile sense.

'The distinctive mark of an educated person is that he possesses a just sense of values. The possession of a standard by which the worthless might be distinguished from the worthy might in the realm of art be called taste; in that of morals, principle; in that of intellect, judgement. Anything specious or shoddy is known to the educated person at once without any proof being needed that this was so. It would be recognised like a bad smell –'

'Like a fart, does he mean?' whispered Johnny, and Lizzie and I suppressed our giggles with no little difficulty.

'And conversely,' droned on Doctor Doolittle, who was inordinately fond of the sound of his own voice, 'the educated person recognises something good instinctively as he would a friendly face. He must have two characteristics – humility, arising from a sense of his own modest place in the general scheme, and reverence, arising from contact with august things which have the right to command it,' he finished off triumphantly.

'Well put, my dear Doctor,' said Reverend Shaw. 'Your words remind me of Professor Webb's little volume on the decline of art. He propounds that the youthful enthusiasm for loveliness in shape and colour, that necessity to reproduce in visible shape our thoughts of the invisible . . .' But I had no desire to hear more of this so I strolled out into the garden which was looking quite bright in the unseasonal bright sunshine.

Lizzie and Sir Gerard Nolan followed me though poor Johnny was trapped between the headmaster and Reverend Shaw.

'You would appreciate a lighter conversation, Miss Everleigh,' smiled the baronet, whose roguish reputation was known to both Lizzie and myself.

'I think that there are matters I find more interesting then modern education theories,' I said with a little smile.

'Well, how about this amusing little anecdote told to me by Lord Totterbridge. It appears that when he was a small child, the Prince of Wales said to a footman: "Frederick, what is the meaning of the word bugger?" "Bugger, Your Royal Highness, why do you ask?"

'"Because I heard my tutor call Taylor the coachman a damned bugger."

'"Ah," said the footman wittily, "a bugger is a person who does a fellow an injury behind his back!"'

This jest put us back into a good humour and we returned to the drawing-room to rescue Johnny who was by now looking somewhat pale and wan. We walked the short distance to the school and took luncheon with the headmaster and members of the staff. I sat next to old Mr Carruthers, the English master who chatted to us about the talented boys we should be seeing in the contest after our meal.

'Take young Ponsonby, for example. What a well-spoken boy who writes the most exquisite verses. I do believe I have one of his efforts here. Sir Gerard, perhaps you would like to read this fine madrigal?'

The baronet took the proferred sheet and glanced down to read the poem. His eyes suddenly brightened and his face creased with mirth as he began to choke with laughter.

'Are you all right, Sir Gerard?' asked Mr Carruthers in some alarm.

'Yes, yes, I am quite recovered,' gasped Sir Gerard. 'A, er, a piece of cheese slipped down the wrong way.'

'How distressing,' said the old gentleman. 'Try taking a sip of water.'

A piece of cheese, I pondered. Sir Gerard was taking fresh fruit as his dessert and he showed no signs of choking until he read young Ponsonby's poem. What had the young scamp written that caused Sir Gerard such merriment. I had to wait only a few seconds for the poem was passed to me straightaway by Sir Gerard who assured me that I would enjoy it.

I must admit that at first I thought the verse rather ordinary, though well enough conceived, although you, dear diary, will immediately see what the cheeky youth had managed to pass forward as serious verses:

Come my love and dwell with me
Under the shade of the greenwood tree,
No one can happier be
Than I shall be if bless'd with thee!

Flowers bloom their brightest there!
Unknown sweet fragrance scents the air
Come, my sweetheard, grant this prayer
Kneeling I now make to thee!

The bell suddenly rang in my brain as I reread the verse and I found it impossible to prevent a smile creeping onto my face.

'It is certainly a spirited and evocative piece of writing,' I managed to say before dissolving into laughter which was echoed by Sir Gerard who lost his battle to keep a straight face.

'Strange,' mused Mr Carruthers. 'Almost everyone who has read the poem finds it amusing. I enjoy the rhythm and the timbre of the words but I fail to find it in any way a source of merriment.'

I am afraid that this set Sir Gerard and I off into further peals of laughter but we were soon silenced by Doctor Doolittle who stood up and announced that the contest for the Everleigh Memorial Prize, which incidentally is a silver cup and a substantial cash award of twenty pounds, would commence in fifteen minutes in the Great Hall.

After this announcement we took the opportunity to take a 'comfort' break. But whilst I was washing my hands (what a strange euphemism we use for describing the simple act of relieving ourselves), and of course without my prior knowledge or consent, Sir Gerard had insisted on offering young Ponsonby a swig of brandy from the hip-flask that the rakish baronet always carried upon his person. Indeed, poor Ponsonby, who was unused to cognac, imbibed more than he should have done and looked somewhat worse for wear as we the judges and contestants took their places for the great debate. The audience was made up of boys from the middle and upper school and in the side, chairs were laid out for a group of the senior masters with a special seat at the front for Johnny who was designated a distinguished guest.

Doctor Doolittle opened the proceedings and introduced Sir Gerard, Reverend Shaw and myself and said a few words about the Everleigh Prize and how important for the mind was the ability to speak in public at a debate with so many present.

'Just what we need,' slurred young Ponsonby softly but in a voice that carried to those of us on the platform and at least the first six rows of our audience. 'Just what we need, a mass debate. Ha, ha, ha!'

Luckily Doctor Doolittle was slightly hard of hearing and missed this interjection though a ripple of laughter cascaded through the rows of boys who had heard the remark. I looked somewhat puzzledly at Sir Gerard and said: 'Is that boy quite well? He is going to be in a lot of trouble if he doesn't take this affair seriously.'

'It's my fault, I'm afraid, I offered him a swig of brandy and I'm afraid it has gone right to his head,' he replied.

'You must confess this if he is caught out,' I insisted and Sir Gerard nodded his agreement.

Meanwhile, the headmaster read out the motion to be discussed, 'that this house does not welcome the decline of reserve amongst women'. It was as well that Ponsonby had been chosen to oppose the motion, I thought to myself, as the respite might clear his head.

The proposer was a tall, strapping, curly-headed youth who possessed a soldierly smartness in his manner. It turned out that he was a scion of General Gower of the 32nd Lancers and he spoke like his father, who I had met at the costume ball I described earlier in these pages, and he spoke in a clipped military manner. I do not remember all he said but he concluded with these words: 'How many women till lately, however talented and well educated they were, ever dreamed of openly writing in the newspapers? To do so would have been considered a few years ago a breach of feminine etiquette. And where in the history of the recent past can one recall the spectacle of women standing upon a public platform and addressing a public assembly? Now they claim an equal right with men to be there.

'These and other innovations have assumed great proportions and I for one do not care to give way to this clamour for absolute equality with men. As far as public life is concerned, I confess I should infinitely prefer that women's assistance should forever be dispensed with, sooner than that by their admission to a share of what hitherto belonged exclusively to men, our women should lose one fraction of the nobility of their sex, or become one jot less mindful of those womanly virtues which are the glory of a civilised country.'

It was now poor Ponsonby's turn to take the stage. He lurched forward and cleared his throat, gave a little burp to the great delight of the boys who had been bored out of their minds by Gower, and began: 'Headmaster, Miss Gerard, Reverend Everleigh, Sir Shaw . . . no, no, thass not quite right . . . Sir Jenny, Reverend Gerard, Miss Shaw . . . no, no, thass not quite right either . . . Miss Reverend, Sir Everleigh, oh what the fuck . . . ladies and gentlespoons, I honour it a great esteem, I mean esteem it a great Everleigh, er, I Shaw it a great Reverend . . .' and the poor boy collapsed into fits of laughter.

By now, the whole audience was howling with glee and before the headmaster, who at first sat transfixed, hardly believing the evidence of his eyes and ears, could drag the unfortunate Ponsonby off the stage, the intoxicated young scamp insisted that he read us another poem:

'There once was a lady named Joy,
Who invented a new kind of toy.
She sugared her quim
Both outside and in
And had it sucked off by a boy!'

Before any further damage could be done, Doctor Doolittle and another master dragged him off the stage and left him in the care of Matron in the sanitarium for the good Doctor, himself never having touched the demon drink, was perhaps fortunately for Ponsonby under the delusion that the boy was suffering from a brainstorm.

For now I shall draw a veil over the rest of that day's proceedings, diary, as time presses on and I must dress myself for the Lord Mayor's Ball at the Mansion House tonight, a grand affair indeed.

But I shall return to that afternoon at Robbelows and will faithfully record the naughty prize I gave Ponsonby and how Sir Gerard and a dormitory maid were found in *flagrante delicto*, etc, etc. So diary, I will continue these candid memoirs at a later date. Enough now, for an author who speaks about his own books is almost as bad as a mother who talks about her own children. I will continue this tale tomorrow.

TO BE CONTINUED